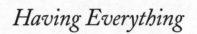

Having Everything

Having Everything

A NOVEL

John L'Heureux

Atlantic Monthly Press
New York

PUBLISHER'S NOTE

This is a work of fiction. Names, characters, places, and incidents either are the product
of the author's imagination or are used fictitiously, and any resemblance to actual per-
sons living or dead, to events, or to locales is entirely coincidental.

ACKNOWLEDGMENT

The author wishes to thank Donald Finkel for permission to reprint a section of his poem
"Three for Robert Rauschenberg," from *A Joyful Noise*, © 1966, by Donald Finkel, published by Atheneum.

Published simultaneously in Canada
Printed in the United States of America

FIRST EDITION

Library of Congress Cataloging-in-Publication Data
L'Heureux, John.
Having everything : a novel / John L'Heureux.
p.   cm.
ISBN 0-87113-763-1
I. Title.
PS3562.H4H38   1999
813'.54—dc21   99-28837

DESIGN BY LAURA HAMMOND HOUGH

Atlantic Monthly Press
841 Broadway
New York, NY 10003

99 00 01 02   10 9 8 7 6 5 4 3 2 1

for
Susan and Marsh McCall

"There must be more to life than having everything."
M. Sendak

Having Everything

ONE

1

Philip Tate was forty-five and he had everything—a distinguished career, a still-beautiful wife, two healthy kids in top schools—and now he had the Goldman Chair. Furthermore he was a good man, essentially.

He was thinking these things, a comfy self-evaluation appropriate to the moment, as that old fool Aspergarter rose to offer his toast. "Philip Tate and his lovely wife Maggie," Aspergarter said, and then blah blah blah, who cares, on and on. Philip looked around the room at his handsome friends in their designer clothes, at the mahogany table and the lead crystal and the heavy sterling, at the deep red walls with the perfectly lit matching Klees, and suddenly he wanted out of here and out of these people's company and out of this straitjacket life that was suffocating him and made him want to rip off his clothes and scream "No" and "No." He smiled instead and tuned into the toast once again. Aspergarter was still droning on—Philip's career as physician, as endocrinologist, as psychiatric voyager blah and blah—but finally, when nobody could stand another second of it, he ground to a halt: "To Philip Tate," he said, "long life, good health, our eternal esteem. Please raise your glass with me to the new Tyler P. Goldman Chair of Psychiatry."

They all raised their glasses and drank.

Philip stood up. He thanked Aspergarter and this splendid group, his friends, colleagues, their spouses, and said that he was speechless—as he often was—but this time he would follow his best instincts and say nothing. "Except thank you, thank you, thank you."

And so it was over. A truly dreadful evening. Then good-byes and thanks and more good-byes and at last they were in their car, driving home.

It was a beautiful June night, cool after a long sunny day, the kind of night that made people remark how lucky they were to live in Boston—in Cambridge, actually—the spring, the fall. But then there were the goddam winters, the ghastly summers . . . well, forget it.

They drove in silence, thinking.

Philip was thinking about the dinner party. From any reasonable point of view, it had been a great success. His friends had been there, some enemies but mostly friends, and they had all been happy for him, or at least most of them had been happy and the rest had pretended, and Maggie had been good, very good in fact, so he too should be happy, shouldn't he? He should be triumphant. But he wasn't.

He smiled at Maggie.

"What?" she said.

"I'm feeling happy," he said. "I'm feeling triumphant."

She looked at him and then at the road that lay ahead of them and said, "You can't complain about me tonight. I was very good."

"I'm feeling happy, I told you. Jesus."

He turned back to the road and after a while she put her hand on his knee, conciliatory.

"You know I love you," he said, but it didn't come out right. It sounded practiced. It sounded as if he was just saying what he had to say. Well, fuck a duck, he had tried to be nice.

They drove on in silence.

A few minutes later they turned down Brattle Street and then a quick left and they were home. Philip said, "Here we are," and glanced over at Maggie. She smiled, looking straight ahead.

"It was nice, Philip," she said. "You should be proud."

She got out of the car and headed straight for the house.

In the kitchen she drank a glass of water and took two aspirins. Philip watched her.

"What?" she said.

"Thank you for tonight," he said.

She looked at him, a question.

"That's all I mean," he said, "just thank you."

"I'm all *right*," she said.

"I know, I know," he said.

He kissed her lightly on the lips and looked into her eyes. She looked away and her eyes wandered to the kitchen cabinet where they kept the breakfast cereal and the liquor.

"Do you want a drink?" he asked. "Let's have a drink."

"If I want one, I'll take one. I don't have to ask your permission."

"I'm gonna have one. Let me make you one."

"Haven't you been toasted enough tonight? You and your goddam Goldman Chair?" She turned and left him.

Philip poured himself a scotch. He could hear the bathwater pounding upstairs. She'd be having her secret drink now, he supposed, or taking her pills, or maybe both. She denied it, of course, but what could you do? There was no shorter route to a fight than asking her if she was okay. What is *that* supposed to mean? she'd say. Or she'd simply turn on that frozen silence she specialized in. There was no dealing with it. And he had no idea when it had begun, or why, or how serious it was.

He sat at the kitchen table and leafed through an old *New Yorker*. He could remember laughing at these cartoons but he couldn't remember why. Someday he should make a study of why people laughed. He knew all about Mounier and the mechanistic theory and the cruelty theory and the inappropriate response theory, but he wondered why they *really* laughed. He had a suspicion that laughter was just another manifestation of despair.

He heard the bathwater being let out. She might come down now and make peace before going to bed. If only he could get through to her. He was a psychiatrist, after all, but that never seemed to make any difference around the house. She was a beautiful woman, very smart, and famous for her wit and charm but above all for her warmth. What on earth had happened to them? He heard her on the stairs and then suddenly she stood in the doorway, her blond hair loose about her shoulders, her face white, and her green eyes glittering with drink. He smiled, nervous.

She kissed him, hard, and he stood up and held her in his arms. He tasted the toothpaste and the gin beneath it and he pressed her body against his own. She was shaking.

"What is it?" he said. "Tell me." He caressed her hair. "I love you, Maggie. You know that."

"Poor Philip," she whispered. They were quiet for a long moment and he deliberately said nothing because perhaps now she might tell him what had come between them, and so he waited. They had everything, their kids and their lives and their health, and they were good-looking, with enough money, and they loved one another—didn't they?—and yet they were wreck-ing it, somehow, in spite of themselves. He waited some more, but she said nothing. "Maggie?" he asked finally, but she only patted his back—it was all over—and gave him a little kiss on the cheek. "You poor thing," she said. "Never mind. It doesn't matter." She collapsed against him for a moment and then, in a distant voice, said, "I'll probably sleep late tomorrow, Philip, I'm awfully tired."

He held her away from him and looked into her eyes. They were empty. She was half asleep already. Pills *and* booze no doubt.

"Good night, love," he said.

She yawned. "Nighty-night," she said, as if she were talking to a baby. She went upstairs to bed, saying, "Nighty-nighty-night."

Philip poured himself another scotch. He got out the ice cubes and deliberately made a racket with the metal tray. Why not? There'd be no waking her now. She'd be dead until the morning.

He stood at the sink and looked at his reflection in the dark window. "Here's to your Chair," he said, lifting his glass. He drank. "And to your lovely wife and kids." He drank again. "And here's to happy memories." For a good half the evening they had discussed recovered memory and poor old Gaspard. What could be nicer, really, than contemplating somebody else's disaster as you downed lamb and polenta and a perfect cabernet? Oh, fuck them all, he hated parties.

The official party—the one at the President's house—had been held a week earlier. The Trustees had been there, and all the big money-givers, and the widow of Tyler P. Goldman himself. There had been endless speeches. Maggie drank a little too much and got surly and made snide comments during the final toast. It was a nightmare.

He poured another drink and went into the tiny family room and flopped on the couch.

This evening's party had been given by Aspergarter, the retiring Dean of the Medical School, as an informal get-together for a group of Philip's close friends. Nice of him to do it. He wasn't obliged to give a party, after all; it was a gesture. Aspergarter had even consulted him about the guest list. The Big A understood how it was: Philip was getting a Chair, and all the heady prestige that went with it, and most of his friends would be jealous, not glad. If he were in trouble, it would be different. You could always find people who would commiserate, and mean it, and maybe even loan you money, but ask them to rejoice? Philip had chosen four couples—the Treanors, the Fioris, the McGuinns, the Stubbses—and the grande dame of psychiatrists, Leona Spitzer. He hadn't included the Kizers, the new people from Duke, but they sort of included themselves, showing up after the meal just as Philip and Maggie were on their way out.

There was a duo. The Kizers. Hal and Dixie. Hal was new to the Medical School and, like Philip, a specialist in depression. Hal seemed to think that meant they had a lot in common, but they had nothing in common. Hal was loud and abrasive. He was sarcastic. There was something wrong with him, something competitive, something sexual maybe. Philip hadn't yet figured it out. Hal always looked—how?—as if he were about to touch his crotch or, worse, touch yours. Philip smiled, recognizing he had hit on something. Scotch could be wonderfully clarifying. Hal was a lecher, nothing very mysterious about that. The wife, though, was something else. Those tight lips, the smirk lingering at the corner of her wide mouth, the tense hands. A sex problem? Insecurity certainly, but what else? Was she simply crazy as a loon? Something. Better not even to think about them.

Philip shrugged deeper into the sofa and stared up at the ceiling. He was forty-five and he had a beautiful wife and two kids and a distinguished career and now he had the Goldman Chair too. He had done everything right. He was a good doctor. He really was. He was sympathetic and he listened and he was tough when he had to be. He believed that life was short and mean and often cruel and that you should do everything you can to make life better for other people. You should give yourself. You should help. You should create good in a rotten world by—he had read a lot of Sartre in college—by doing one good thing, and then another, and then another. He had done this. He had always chosen the best over the second-best, no matter how hard the choice.

And he had good kids. They were great kids. Emma was at Berkeley, a sophomore, and Cole had just finished first-year medicine at Hopkins. Cole was brainier and more studious. He didn't have Emma's sense of humor. But they were great kids, both of them. Cole was more like his mother.

He thought about when he himself was a kid. The house-breaker of Brookline, Mass.

Tonight at dinner they had talked about recovered memory because of old Gaspard's situation. Gaspard was a former Dean of the Medical School who was being sued by his thirty-five-year-old daughter for molesting her when she was in grammar school. She had recovered the lost memory during psycho-therapy, she claimed—therapy that Gaspard had paid for—and she brought charges against him that she intended to pursue in court. Everybody at the table had an opinion about recovered memory, and a story to illustrate it, but only Roberto Fiori claimed to have had such an experience himself. On his wed-ding night, he said, he had approached the bed where Isabella lay waiting for him, her hair spread out against the pillow, and a shaft of moonlight had fallen across the bed . . .

"A *shaft* of moonlight?" Beecher Stubbs asked, and Calvin Stubbs said, "What about all this hair spread out on the pillow?" and then Leona Spitzer said, "Come on, Roberto, it sounds more like *True Romance* than recovered memory," and that was where Philip had stopped listening. He had his own secret memory.

In high school, on a bet, he had broken into a neighbor's house.

A bunch of guys had been shooting the shit one day after gym class, talking about last year's senior class president, who had been arrested for breaking and entering. Ralphie was say-ing that he must have been shit-stupid not to know he'd get caught and everybody agreed except Philip. "You don't have to get caught," Philip said, "you only have to use your head." And within a couple minutes he had bet each of them ten bucks he could break into a house and not get caught. He'd bring back proof, he said. Two nights later he let himself into Ralphie's house—he knew they kept the spare key under the pot of hydrangeas—and stole his autographed baseball. The next day when they were all gathered around their lockers, Philip said, "Hey, shithead, is this your ball?" and, as the others watched, he turned the ball over in his hands, studying it, and then passed it around the group. The ball was signed by Mickey Mantle and everybody knew it was Ralphie's. "Yours?" Philip said. "Or should I just keep it?" Ralphie paid up at once and, reluctantly, so did the others.

That was the end of it, or so everybody thought. Days passed, and then a week passed, and each night Philip lay awake thinking of that moment when he had paused at the back door of Ralphie's house, listening to the silence, waiting for something to happen.

He had inserted the key, waited a moment, turned it, and then slowly, slowly pushed the door inward. It creaked just a little and he paused, his heart banging and an empty feeling in his head, but the silence had continued and he stepped inside and eased the door shut behind him. He stood for a moment in the familiar kitchen, his eyes adjusting to the dark. The refrigerator suddenly began to hum and he stepped back quickly, knocking into an empty six-pack of Coke that somebody had shoved behind the door. The bottles rattled loudly in the still house. For a long time he stood motionless, listening, but there was no other sound. He laughed softly. He felt giddy because of what he was about to do.

He walked through the kitchen and down the hall to the staircase. He stopped and listened again. The house was very dark and it smelled faintly of soap. He had never noticed that before. He put one foot on the bottom step. It creaked, as he knew it would, but he put his full weight on it and then stopped. Nothing. He took the next step, and the next, and in a couple seconds he was up the stairs, feeling his way along the wall to Ralphie's room. The wallpaper was pebbly here, with lots of tiny bumps. He stopped outside the open door. He could hear snoring from the big bedroom at the end of the hall and from Ralphie's room he heard a thin asthmatic wheeze. He stepped inside. He could barely make out Ralphie's face on the pillow, his mouth open, his head thrown back. He walked to the foot of the bed and stared at him. He was tempted to say "Boo!" or make ghost sounds or just keep staring into Ralphie's face until he woke up and hollered. He liked the idea of scaring the shit out of him. Somewhere in the neighborhood a dog barked once and then stopped. Downstairs the refrigerator stopped humming. You could hear everything, anything. He looked around the room and in a crack of light from the window he saw Ralphie's desk and on it the baseball signed by Mickey Mantle. The ball would be perfect.

In another second he had taken the ball and was in the corridor on his way to the stairs. There was a cough from the big bedroom and then a different kind of silence. He heard rustling noises and the creak of bedsprings and then heavy feet on the hardwood floor. Still he stood there, motionless, waiting to be discovered. Then he heard loud peeing from the master bathroom and, grateful, he descended the stairs quickly, lightly, and under the sound of the flushing toilet he let himself out the kitchen door, testing afterward to see that it was locked. He put the key under the pot of hydrangeas. And he was home, as he thought, free.

That's how it had been on the night he stole the baseball, and every night afterward he lay awake reliving the sensations of it all, one by one. The pause inside the kitchen door, the rattling Coke bottles, the creak of the bottom stair, the smell of soap, the feel of his fingers on the pebbly wall, the snoring from the parents' room and Ralphie's wheezing, and then the crazy feeling of standing in the room with somebody asleep and you knowing and he not knowing and then not scaring the shit out of him even though you could if you wanted to but instead just stealing the baseball that proved you were there, and then leaving, while somebody was up and awake and peeing right next door, and you were in their house and they didn't know it and you just left, stepping out into the cool dark, no harm done.

No harm done, that was the big thing. Because what, after all, was wrong with it? Nothing, really. It was just fun, it was funny. And so why not do it again?

But he knew that was crazy and he put it out of his mind. Still, what harm?

He broke into the house next door to Ralphie's, though it wasn't really breaking in. He just *let* himself in, with a key; it was definitely not breaking and entering. This time was more scary than the first, because he had known Ralphie's house well, but this one was altogether new to him and he didn't know his way around. All he knew was that they didn't have a dog. He counted on that. He closed the door behind him and stood inside the little kitchen entryway and he was suddenly paralyzed with fear. What was he doing? What if he got caught? If he'd been caught in Ralphie's house, he could have said he was just playing a trick and they'd have believed him, but in this house they'd be convinced he was trying to rob them. He stood in the entryway, trembling, and he promised himself, or maybe God, that if he got out of here safely, he'd never do anything this crazy again. He let himself out, put the key back under the mat, and ran all the way home.

It was crazy, insane. Never again.

The next night he went back to the same house, walked through all the downstairs rooms, touching the furniture, the walls, the potted plants on the windowsills. He felt no panic this time. It was exciting, because you might get caught, and it was sexy in a way he couldn't quite explain to himself, but mostly it was—well—just fun. And harmless. He didn't take anything and he didn't damage anything. He just walked around inside the house, he helped himself to a piece of hard candy from a dish on the dining room table, he sat down in front of the blank TV and pretended he lived there. I mean, what was so bad about it, he said to himself, what was the big deal anyhow? But he told nobody what he'd done, not Ralphie or the gang or even the priest in confession.

He put it out of his conscious mind; it was just something that had happened once—well, twice, if you counted Ralphie's house—and he refused to think about it. Two weeks went by, and then a third, and when it crossed his mind, he couldn't believe he had ever done it. A month later, though, he gave it another try. It was easy. People in his neighborhood left keys under the mat, in potted plants, on the ledge above the door. Everybody was trusting or just careless. Once, during a heat spell in July, he had found a door ajar.

Then, in August, he was caught in the Sanderses' house. He was letting himself out the back door, just a little excited, just a little bit triumphant, when he was suddenly confronted by Dr. Sanders, who was on his way in. "Philip?" he asked. "Can that be Philip?" They looked at one another blankly for a moment and then Philip smiled and said, "Hi, Dr. Sanders. I guess the jig is up." As usual, he was lucky. Dr. Sanders was a professional colleague of his father's, they worked together in the same medical complex, and though Sanders didn't call the police, he did talk to Philip's father the next day to urge that the boy see a psychiatrist. And who better than himself?

So Philip saw Dr. Sanders once a week, professionally, and by October he had come to realize that these night visits to other people's houses were simply a manifestation of his need to matter, his desire to be special, his longing for intimacy. And what else? he wondered, though he did not raise that question. He and Dr. Sanders became friends as Philip entered his new and more stable years. He put his housebreaking phase so completely behind him that he almost believed it had never happened. His parents never mentioned it again, nor did Dr. Sanders, and so far as his friends knew, he had done it only once, on a bet, as a joke on Ralphie.

Philip studied more, his grades shot up, his teachers began to notice that he was quite a talented young man. He might eventually become a doctor like his father, or he might enter the priesthood, or he might—if it weren't for a certain natural shyness—find a place in politics. Certainly he was going to become something interesting. And he did. He married right after college—with no mention, of course, of his career as a housebreaker—he studied medicine, and he moved to Chicago, where he got a very good job at the university hospital. In a few years he began to specialize in endocrinology. Which led him—naturally, he felt—to psychiatry and the physiology of depression. Then a job offer at Harvard—it would mean that at last he had everything, so who could say no? And now he had a Chair. Oh, let us never forget the Chair. Ta-daa! Not to mention the whispers that he might be the next Dean of the Medical School.

"Thus far, my life," Philip said aloud, and smiled to himself. He was lying on the couch in the small family room, remembering, with what seemed like pleasure. He reached for his glass, which was empty, and then he reached for the remote control and flicked on the TV. Test patterns, lousy movies, infomercials. He flicked it off.

He stood up and looked around the room. Who lived here? What could you tell from just looking? They had taste, probably a little money, they liked to read. Furniture getting a little shaggy. But two very good McKnight prints. He got up and walked into the kitchen and from there to the big family room they used only when the kids were home. He looked at the dining room and the living room. Formal, but not too formal. Lived in.

He went into the kitchen and made himself another drink. Scotch. Easy on the water. This was absurd, of course. He would have a headache tomorrow, but what the hell, it was a celebration. They had given him a Chair. Because he was a good psychiatrist, a good teacher, a good husband and father and citizen. He did not fuck his colleagues' wives or children. He did not seduce and abandon patients. He did not steal.

But he did break into houses. Or he had. Once upon a time. When he was fifteen. And he had never forgotten it, not really.

He stood at the kitchen sink and looked out the window. It was a dark night, very little moon, and there was a light breeze. He could go for a walk. He could clear his head. Sure.

He finished his drink, turned out the light, and then went back to the window and stared out into the dark. It was chilly at this hour. He'd need a jacket if he went for a walk. And he'd have to change his clothes.

"No," he said aloud. He would not go out for a walk. That was crazy. That was asking for trouble.

He would go to bed. He moved quickly to the front room and mounted the stairs and looked into the bedroom. Maggie was in deep sleep. "Maggie?" he said, and there was no response at all. He took off his suit and hung it in the closet. He hung up his tie, his shirt. He tossed his underwear in the hamper and put on his pajamas. He got into bed.

His heart was beating very fast. "No," he said again, and looked over to see if Maggie had stirred, but she was out, completely gone. "No," he whispered, but he got up and got dressed in his jeans and running shoes and, without another glance at Maggie, left their bedroom and went downstairs. He took his black windbreaker from the hall closet, his keys from the tray on the refrigerator, and stepped outside. He locked the door behind him.

It was colder now. He felt good. He would not go for a walk after all, he would go for a little drive. Insomniacs did that all the time. So why shouldn't he?

He drove through Harvard Square to Mass. Ave. and then, without even thinking, he hit the Alewife Brook Parkway and decided to take it—why not?—and in a short while he was in

Winchester, very near the Aspergarters' house. It was a wealthy
neighborhood with big houses and wide lawns and low fieldstone walls. And, no doubt, security systems to protect the Klees
and the Mirós and the Mondrians. All the lights were out. He
drove slowly past the house and made a bunch of left turns and
passed in front of it again. What dull secrets lurked behind the
banal masks of the Aspergarters? Would anyone care? Would
anyone want to know? He turned back toward home and as he
passed from Winchester to Cambridge he noticed again, as he
always did, the sudden change from real wealth to middle-class
affluence, from the world of Klees and security systems to
McKnight prints and keys under the mat. The difference annoyed the hell out of some people. It meant nothing to him.
Money was something he couldn't understand as a value in itself. It had nothing to do, finally, with who you were. He was in
Harvard Square heading for Brattle Street when, for no reason
at all, no reason he could think of anyhow, he circled back again
and drove out to Winchester. The Kizers lived in a new development. Big showy houses, with high walls and foolproof security systems. And dogs, certainly. He turned left on Meadow and
then right on Woodlawn, and drove past the Kizers' house. He'd
never been inside, but he knew the development because he
and Maggie had once thought of moving out here, but Maggie
said it was too expensive, what with the kids going off to college, and so they had stayed in Cambridge.

A dim light was burning downstairs. He looked at his
watch—3 A.M. Could Hal be working? It seemed unlikely. He
doubted if Hal ever worked, really. Hal had other interests. He
drove to the end of Woodlawn, a cul-de-sac, and parked several
houses down on the opposite side of the street. He walked back
to the house, through the huge open gate to the driveway, and
from the safety of the evergreens he peered into the front window. It was Hal's study all right, but nobody was there. Several
books lay open on the desk.

He went down the long curving driveway and around to the back. There was a fake Tudor portico and a sheltered entrance and a door with a long glass panel. Anybody could break in here in thirty seconds. He looked for wiring, a panel of some kind with buttons on it, some minimal security system at least. He knew there had to be one, but he could see no sign of it. If he forced the door and an alarm went off, he'd have a fucking stroke. He put his hand on the doorknob. Nothing. His heart was beating double time. What the hell. He turned the knob slowly, he leaned hard against the door, he waited for the screech of the alarm. Nothing. Not a sound. Nor did the door give.

He looked under the mat. No key. And there were no potted plants either. He felt the ledge above the door. Sure enough.

He took a quick look around him. The night was cold and quiet. Not a sound. The smell of mint from the side garden. He breathed in the scent of it and held his breath.

He should go home now, right now. He should get back into bed and thank the gods he had escaped from a crazy pointless act that could change his life forever. It was madness. It was lunacy.

He slipped the key in the lock, turned it, and the door opened. There was no alarm. There was nothing. He stepped inside.

The house was very quiet.

2

Maggie was in deep sleep and then, a second later, she was fully awake. This had been happening a lot lately. It had something to do with the pills she took.

Philip lay beside her in bed. He was sleeping on his back, his hands folded across his chest like an Etruscan death figure. He had a gorgeous profile: hooded eyes, a hawkish kind of nose, a wide full mouth. His good looks still surprised her. To be truthful, what surprised her was that somebody who looked like Philip would have married her. He was short, though, and that's all he thought of when he considered his own looks. He had no sense of his appearance or of his accomplishments or even of who he was. Or of who she was. Instantly she was swamped by one of those irrational waves of hatred—she couldn't breathe, she couldn't think, she wanted to escape—and then, just as quickly, it passed, and she was left feeling empty and guilt-ridden and afraid to be discovered. Poor Philip. She looked over at him. If he only knew what he was stuck with.

Had she been impossible last night? Well, today would be different. Today would mark the beginning of a whole new life for them. She would cut down on the pills. She would stop drinking altogether. She would . . . Well, no more resolutions, she would just do it.

She slipped out of bed and put on her robe and slippers. Philip was sleeping soundly. She did her teeth and ran a comb through her hair. She put on a touch of lipstick. On her way from the bathroom she noticed his jeans on the floor next to the bed, his ratty old black windbreaker on top of them. He must have gone for a walk last night. She hung up his jeans and jacket. She looked at him and saw that he was not wearing pajamas. He always wore pajamas because otherwise he caught a chill. Poor old Philip. He must have sat up half the night drinking and then, after his walk, just tumbled into bed. He'd have a filthy hangover when he woke. She was lucky, she never had hangovers.

She went downstairs and put on the coffee. She leaned against the counter and looked out the window. A black squirrel streaked across the patio and a moment later a fat white cat appeared from the bushes and went off in the direction of the squirrel. A bird called, complaining.

"Nature," Maggie said, "red in tooth and claw."

Which brought her back to last night's party. She had been very good. She had drunk only two glasses of wine and she had made conversation, or at least she had tried, and she had gazed lovingly at Philip while Aspergarter praised him in that condescending way of his. "Philip Tate's distinction. His brilliance. His generosity and his dedication and his wisdom. And, of course, his lovely wife." Lovely wife, my ass. She could be a chimpanzee for all they noticed. These smug, self-satisfied, arrogant, detestable men. She hated them and their condescension. And the women shrinks were even worse. She hated them all.

Without thinking, she shook two aspirins from the bottle on the counter and swallowed them, not bothering with water.

The coffee was still not ready. She began to tidy up. She put the bottle of scotch in the cereal cabinet and ran a damp sponge over the table and then wiped it down with a paper towel. She took the glasses from the counter and put them in the dishwasher. She scoured the sink. The coffee was ready now and she filled a cup and took it into the little family room. She turned on the television. Cartoons: it must be Saturday. There was a full glass of something on the end table next to the couch. Scotch, with almost no water. She put down her coffee and took a sip of the scotch. She made a face—it was very strong—and she lay down on the couch.

She flipped through the channels until she came to a program on home improvement. Renovation plans were being carefully explained by a middle-aged man and a younger woman, blond of course, both of them beautifully groomed and wearing jeans. They were going to tear out the walls of an old farmhouse to bring in light and air. Very nice.

She took another sip of the scotch and curled up to watch them work.

They were going to replace a blank wall, the man explained, and install a row of windows looking out onto what would eventually become a duck pond. He pointed to an artist's rendering of how the place would look when it was all done. Pale greens and yellows and a lot of white. Light and air. Lovely. Lovely.

She stretched out more comfortably on the couch and watched them attack the plaster walls with crowbar and chisels. She took another little sip of scotch. She turned the sound lower. She closed her eyes and saw the lovely greens and yellows of the duck pond and the grass.

It was all so peaceful. So quiet. So good.

She fell asleep, a smile on her lips.

Upstairs in their bedroom Philip too was asleep. He was hot and uncomfortable. He pushed the lumped-up blanket from his neck and rolled over on his side. He was rising, reluctantly, to the surface of consciousness and he made one last attempt to dive deeper, to stay unconscious. Suddenly he sneezed.

He opened his eyes and glanced at the other side of the bed. She was up already. He could smell coffee and there was light streaming in the window. And then the pain struck, a hammer blow between his eyes. That party. The tension generated by Aspergarter's praise. The worry about Maggie and what she might drink, what she might do. His head was pounding. He would never drink again. Never. He needed coffee. He would have to—somehow—drag himself out of bed.

Only then did he realize he was naked. He made a half-hearted thrusting motion with his hips and ran his hand down his chest and stomach to his crotch. In the old days he and Maggie would have got it on right away. Hangover or not. They'd let the coffee wait and just do it, slowly, gently, and then with a nice hard fierceness, and afterward they'd lie there getting their breath back, sticky and satisfied and exhausted. He smiled to himself despite the headache. Maybe they'd get it all back one of these days. Maybe this was the middle-aged adjustment everybody went through. It happened. You had to live through it. Life was the best thing going, if you considered the alternative.

He sneezed again. Why was he not wearing pajamas?

And then it struck him. He had gone to bed wearing pajamas but he had taken them off and put on his jeans and his black windbreaker and gone for a drive in the car. At two in the morning. Or three. He had driven over to Winchester and then around back streets until he found himself at the Aspergarters' house. He had started home, but instead he doubled back to the Kizers' place. There was a light on in Hal's study. He had parked the car. He had searched for a key beneath the mat and above the door frame and he had found the key. He had turned it in the lock and stepped inside. There had been no alarm.

Philip covered his face and groaned.

He couldn't have done it, it was a nightmare, it was unthinkable. He would *not* think about it. It did not, it could not have happened.

Nevertheless, he is back at the Kizers' door, he has pushed it open and now he steps inside. The house is very quiet.

He is in some kind of entryway. It is large, with storage cabinets and a washer and dryer and a huge tile planter that holds umbrellas and walking sticks. It's like an English mudroom where you'd keep your hiking clothes for rambles over the moors. There's a huge wrought-iron birdcage, empty. A green leather bench with golf shoes lying on it. On the walls there are framed prints, probably hunting scenes. He can't make out the pictures in this dark.

He opens the door to the kitchen and the refrigerator begins to hum. This always happens when you break into a house. It's a friendly sound once you get used to it. He smiles. A night-light on the counter shows him the kitchen is white: white tile, white cabinets, white stove and refrigerator, and a gleaming white work island with a white marble top, and a bank of fluorescent lights, also white. An obsessive's kitchen.

There is a door to the right that leads to a corridor and Hal's study and another door to the left that opens to the dining room. He chooses the dining room. Rosewood furniture, a table that seats twelve or more, a china tureen in the center, expensive and hideous. Double doors stand open to the living room. It is huge. A grand piano dominates one corner of the room. There is a central fireplace with couches on either side, matching wing chairs, some expensive-looking little tables. Lamps everywhere. And there are dark wood bookshelves all along the fireplace wall. Another seating area, with couches again and fat club chairs, looks out on a walled patio. He goes to the French doors and grasps the knob. The doors are unlocked. Do they think they can keep out intruders merely because the patio has a high wall?

He steps away from the doors and bumps into the writing desk. A bronze ashtray rattles and he steadies it. It has startled him, and he stands there listening. Not a sound. Nothing.

He is about to retrace his steps when he notices that beyond the piano is another door that gives onto a sunroom that also overlooks the patio. There are windows on three walls of this room and, even though it is dark outside, the windows admit a dim light that lets him see the wicker couch and the three chairs and the green and white arabesques of the Chinese carpet on the floor. And he sees too that someone is sitting in one of those chairs.

He is paralyzed. He cannot move, but he sucks in his breath suddenly, horribly, and the noise is very loud in the room. He wants to turn and run.

"Well?" the person says, and he recognizes Dixie's voice. She is sitting with her back to him, looking out on the patio.

He says nothing. He cannot speak and he cannot move.

"Well, are you home for the night? Or have you got some other whore waiting for you?" She sounds very drunk. "You shit," she says.

He takes a step toward her then—why, he doesn't know, because his only desire is to run—and her hand flies up to protect her face and she shouts, "Don't! No!" and she begins to cry. She is drunk and crazy and she buries her face in her lap, her hands flapping to keep him away. He realizes finally that she thinks he is Hal, that she has no idea who he is, that he is safe, he is saved.

At that moment she turns and looks at him.

He runs.

Surely this did not happen. It couldn't have happened.

Philip rolled over on his stomach and buried his face in the pillow. "I won't think, I won't think, I won't think," he said aloud, and pressed the pillow hard into his face to smother the awful memory of it: the key on the ledge, Dixie flapping her hands and shouting "No, no," and then his dash through the living room and the dining room, banging against chairs, tumbling into the china tureen, and out into the black night, alone.

Driving home fast, reckless, he had for one moment thought of suicide, and he thought of it now as he lay with his face in the pillow. The disgrace for his family. For poor Maggie and the kids. For the hospital, too, since they have just given him a Chair. "Goldman Professor of Psychiatry accused of breaking and entering. Theft of art objects. Attempted rape." He could see it on the front page of the *Boston Globe*. He held his breath and listened to the pulse pounding in his brain. Stroke time. Or at least a cerebral hemorrhage. He got up slowly and made his way to the bathroom.

In the shower he leaned against the tile and let the hot water beat down on him, hard. He refused to think. He would wash and dress and go down to breakfast. He would get through the day. And the week. And the rest of his life, disgraced or not. He always did what he had to do. That's what life meant: seeing your duty and doing it. And if you fucked up every twenty-five years or so and broke into a house or two, you took the consequences and you got in step and you marched. He always had. And he would.

He put on his chinos and his yellow shirt and went down to join Maggie.

She was not in the kitchen. He looked out the window and his head throbbed at the brightness of the light. She was not in the garden either. He poured himself some coffee and stood drinking it. Maybe she had gone out. Or maybe she knew about last night. Again the blood rushed to his head and he saw Dixie Kizer sitting there in the dark, drunk, and the pain gathered behind his eyes. But there was no way Maggie could know. Unless Dixie had seen him.

He took his coffee into the family room.

Maggie was lying there asleep, peaceful, beautiful. She opened her eyes and smiled at him, and when he did not smile back, she looked away.

"I fell asleep," she said, and sat up.

He was looking at the glass of scotch, half empty now, on the table beside the couch. She looked at it too.

"I didn't touch it," she said. "I didn't."

"I know," he said, but he sounded as if he didn't mean it. He was overwhelmed then by his hypocrisy and his failure and his sense that she was exposed and broken and pitiful and *he* was passing judgment on her. It was all backward. It was wrong and horribly unfair. He was a liar and a cheat and she was the victim. He bent down to kiss her.

"I don't want to lose you, ever," he said, and they embraced, hard, with a touch of desperation. They clung to one another for a long moment, and then for another moment that in the old days would have led them up the stairs to bed. But there was something between them now that was no longer simply love and, slowly, awkwardly, they pulled away.

"We can eat out," Maggie said. "We can have breakfast at Town Line. Do you want to?"

"Winchester?" he said. "Isn't that kind of far?"

"They've got that great French toast you like," she said.

And so they put the past night behind them and dressed and went out—a happily married couple—to have breakfast at Town Line in Winchester.

3

Hal Kizer came down the stairs and went into the sunroom to see if Dixie was still there. She was asleep in the yellow chaise longue, her body twisted uncomfortably, her head thrown back. She would have a sore neck when she woke up. And her customary hangover.

There was a half-empty bottle of bourbon on the floor by her chair and an empty glass lay turned over on its side. He picked them up and took them out to the kitchen. He put on a pot of coffee.

Last night had been his monthly sex seminar up in the city and he was feeling relaxed this morning, all the tensions drained out. He never felt bad about these seminars—no guilt, no anxiety, no discomfort of any kind—and now and then he wondered if he might be some kind of sociopath. An educated one, naturally, and a sympathetic one as well. But, by definition, a man without a conscience. It was possible, though not likely, because sex had nothing to do with a sense of right and wrong, not even rough sex, not even really rough sex.

He went back to the sunroom to look in on Dixie. She was still sleeping. A silk shawl lay across her feet and trailed onto the floor. He shook it out and then carefully drew it up from her legs to her shoulders. She woke. His face was bent over hers and her eyes grew large with fear, but he smiled at her. He kissed her softly on the mouth. "Hi," he whispered. "How's my girl?"

She shifted on the chaise and put her hand up to her neck.
"Sore neck?"

"Mm."

"I'll get you a Tylenol."

"No," she said.

He returned in a moment with a glass of tomato juice and two Tylenol. She swallowed the pills and took a sip of the tomato juice.

He sat down on the edge of the chaise, facing her, and smoothed the dark hair back from her brow. She still had on all her makeup.

"I'm a mess," she said.

"You're my mess," he said. He always felt tender toward her after his sex seminars.

"I had the strangest dream. It was awful."

"What about?"

"I don't remember. I just remember it was awful."

He looked at her, smiling easily. He was very relaxed.

She said, "It was about you, I think."

"Wish fulfillment? Or night fears?"

"What do you mean?"

"I mean, did you kill me or did I kill you?"

"It was about you and it wasn't about you." She shook her head. "I can't get it."

"Don't think about it. Just let it come."

She closed her eyes. She was in a dark room, asleep, alone. But then somebody was there, watching her. Hal was there. He was angry. He was about to hit her. She opened her eyes and he was smiling at her.

"Got it?"

She lifted her hand to his face, stubbly because he hadn't yet shaved, and she thought, Why can't he always be like this, why can't I always love him like this?

He kissed her again, this time on the forehead.

"Get a shower," he said, "and I'll bring you coffee while you dress. And then we'll go out to breakfast, what do you say?"

She clung to him and he held her dutifully and after a while he pushed her away. She was crying, grateful.

He wanted to say, Snap out of it, but he was being quite consciously patient, and so he said nothing. He gave her little soothing pats on the back. "Okay," he said, "it's okay," and then she went upstairs to shower and he was free to have his cup of coffee and flip through the latest *New England Journal of Medicine*. Stern stuff, this.

After a while he poured a cup of coffee and took it upstairs to Dixie. He put it on the dresser and glanced into the bathroom. She was standing there naked, blow-drying her hair, and when she saw him she covered herself with a towel. He smiled at her and said, "There's your coffee," and went downstairs to wait.

He was deep into an essay on carcinogens when she appeared, in white slacks and a red and white striped shirt, looking fresh and young and sexy, all part of the illusion.

"Denny's," he said, "or Town Line?"

"Town Line," she said.

"Town Line it is," he said.

4

It was inevitable that they would meet in the parking lot at Town Line. It was inevitable that they would say what a nice party it had been last night, what wonderful hosts the Aspergarters were, how right and just that Philip should have the Goldman Chair and all the perks that went with it. It was inevitable that Hal would insist on their all having breakfast together. A postcelebration celebration. A good start to a great day.

They sat and the waiter brought coffee and took their orders—French toast all around—and they were left on their own. Nobody knew how to begin. Luckily, Calvin and Beecher Stubbs came in and were seated on the upper level, so for a while they talked about Calvin and Beecher. Then they talked about the Fioris, who always had Saturday breakfast here but hadn't come in yet this morning. Finally, inevitably, they talked about the Tate kids, Cole and Emma, who would be coming home soon for a quick visit before taking off for the summer. Cole had a research assistantship at Hopkins doing blood work, HIV stuff. Emma was going to some Greek island to intern as a dirt-sifter on an archeological dig. Great kids, both of them. No drugs. A little too serious maybe, but who could complain?

Good kids led to the subject of bad kids, and it was only another minute before they were talking about old Gaspard and his daughter's lawsuit and the whole business of recovered memory.

"It's a crock, if you ask me," Hal said. "It's just irresponsible therapy. You suggest, you imply, you create the desire for approval, and you give that approval as soon as the 'memory'—in quotes—veers toward anything sexual. And it's only a small step from a sexual memory to the 'memory'—in quotes—of sexual molestation. Am I right?"

"Hmm," Philip said. He was watching Dixie, who sat there silent, a smirk at the corner of her mouth. Was it a smirk?

"I feel bad for the Gaspards," Maggie said.

"And then of course there's this cult of Victimhood. With a capital V. Everybody wants to be a victim today. The blacks, the Chicanos, the Indians—Native Americans, I mean—well, they *are* victims, but they revel in it, is the point. It's an excuse for not doing anything with their lives. It's an excuse for just collecting welfare and bitching and moaning and, you know, etcetera, etcetera. There's no shame attached to it anymore. They go on television and talk about it. It's a way of being special. My point is that the whole notion of heroism has been supplanted by victimhood. Rape victims, molestation victims, minority bias victims . . . I suppose it's only a matter of time until we have skinhead victims. There aren't any victimizers anymore, there's just victims."

The waiter came with their breakfasts and it looked for a moment as if Hal had been derailed, but he tasted his French toast and returned to the attack.

"Of course, you can't say any of that, publicly anyhow, because it marks you as a racist or a sexist or a supremacist or whatever. I think it's a crock," he said. "So what do *you* think?"

"Of?"

"Of recovered memory. Of the Gaspard girl. I mean, you must know her. I've never laid eyes on her, thank God, or I suppose she'd be accusing me as well."

"She's a very quiet young woman, as I recall. None of us really knew her." Philip looked to Maggie but she had nothing to say.

"It makes me uncomfortable," he said, "this whole business of recovering memory. I'm sure that memories can be suppressed, repressed, completely 'forgotten,' and then surface all of a sudden at some crisis moment. There's no question that it happens. But it's awfully hard to believe you can completely forget something as extreme as molestation. I *know* it happens and even I find it hard to believe. But then, I was never molested."

"So far as you remember," Maggie said.

"So far as I remember," Philip said, and they all laughed, a little nervously.

Philip looked at Dixie and raised his eyebrows. Was she going to say something finally or just sit there with that look on her face?

Dixie cleared her throat and started to speak but then stopped.

"And what do *you* think?" Philip asked.

"Oh," Dixie said. "I don't . . . I mean, I'm not qualified . . . ," and she looked over at Hal and then down at her plate. The smirk disappeared. It had not been a smirk after all. It was tension, perhaps even fear.

"Well, say *something*," Hal said, "for Christ's sake, you're not a mute."

Dixie said, "Oh," and then nothing. There was a little silence and Maggie said, "Dixie probably thinks the same as I think."

Dixie looked up at her.

"That recovered memory is better left to the professionals. They're the ones that make their livings off it."

"Yes," Dixie said.

"The spouses just clean up after them."

"Yes," Dixie said.

"The dutiful spouses," Maggie said. "What would life be without them?"

Dixie said nothing.

"Which means?" Hal said.

"We put up with you," Maggie said, and smiled. "We listen to all the things you remember and we remember all the things you forget—and there are plenty of things you *want* to forget—and we remain mindful, always, that you're the still point of the turning world." She put her hand over Philip's hand. "Isn't that right, sweet?"

"Whew!" Hal said, and began to study her.

"And we love you for it, of course," Maggie said, and to Dixie, "Don't we?"

Dixie was just looking at her.

"Well, we do. " Maggie lifted her cup of coffee in a mock toast and took a sip.

Nobody knew what to say next. The waiter brought more coffee.

"I like that they give you more coffee before you ask," Dixie said.

"I do too," Maggie said.

Another silence.

Hal was still studying Maggie. "So," he said, "you must be real pleased with Philip's Chair. It's quite a thing at . . . What are you, Philip? Forty? Fifty?"

"Forty-five."

"Forty-five and you've got a Chair of Psychiatry at the foremost teaching hospital in the country?"

"It's wonderful," Dixie said. "I think it's just wonderful."

"Not too shabby," Hal said, turning back to Maggie. "That must make you feel real good. *I* don't have a Chair."

"But you have a supportive wife," Maggie said.

"And beautiful too," Philip said.

"But not a Chair."

"Maybe . . . um . . . when you're forty-five . . . ," Dixie said.

"I may be dead when I'm forty-five. *You* may be dead when I'm forty-five."

"How old *are* you?" Maggie said. "With such a young wife."

He looked at her. "Thirty-something," he said.

"He's thirty-eight," Dixie said.

"And do you like it here? Without a Chair?"

"He's thirty-eight," Dixie said again.

"We heard you," Hal said. "Nobody cares."

"And I'm thirty-one," Dixie said.

"My, my," Hal said. "She speaks and everything."

"*And* I'm a second wife."

"A rich second wife, be it known," Hal said. "Don't forget rich."

"And beautiful." Maggie smiled at her.

But Dixie was too upset to notice the smile and got up quickly and left for the women's room.

"Is she going to be okay?" Maggie asked.

"She's tense a lot," Hal said.

"Yes. I should think."

"It doesn't mean anything."

"It doesn't *mean* anything?" Maggie looked at him with something like contempt. "Thus spake the psychiatrist?"

"All right. Okay. What it means is this: one, she's sensitive about being a second wife; two, she had a few drinks too many last night; three, your sympathy or pity, whatever, has made her bold for the moment and she's decided to take me on in public. It's not a role she can handle. She crumbles too easily. Dixie is not what she seems."

"I'll see if she's all right," Maggie said, and left the table.

"Women," Hal said. "Freud was right."

"Maybe you could go easier," Philip said. "That was a pretty tough exchange."

"Maybe I could," Hal said.

"So." Philip toyed with his knife and fork. "How *do* you like it here? Better than Tufts? The same?"

"Better, worse, all teaching hospitals are the same. What I like here is the proximity of the city."

"Boston? Or New York?"

"Well, both. But I meant Boston."

"Opera?"

"No. I can't take opera. Dixie likes opera."

"The Symphony?"

"Sex, as a matter of fact."

"Ah, sex."

Hal imitated the carefully neutral tone. "Ah, sex," he said. And then, "I can explain. I'd like to explain, in fact. I'd be curious to hear your take on it."

Philip put his hands up, palms out. Not interested.

Maggie and Dixie returned to the table. Dixie's eyes were red, but she and Maggie were chatting as if nothing had happened. They sat down.

"I'd like more coffee," Dixie said.

"Me too." Philip motioned to the waiter.

"Mmm, yum," Maggie said.

"I think it's just wonderful that they've honored you with this Chair," Dixie said. "You have everything. Maggie, and your kids, and I'm sure you have a lovely home. I think it's wonderful."

"Well, thank you," Philip said.

"House," Hal said, "not home."

"Oh, I'm sure theirs is a home," Dixie said, and she kept on looking at Philip. "You even have a wonderful face."

Philip blushed a little.

"It is. It's . . . wonderful."

"She likes 'wonderful,' you see," Hal said.

"It's kind and it's strong and it's—I don't know—familiar in some way."

The waiter, pouring coffee, paused to look at Philip's face.

"Familiar?" Maggie said. "I think it's kind of unique. That nose?"

"Can we please talk about something other than my face?" Philip said.

"I'm sorry," Dixie said. "I didn't mean . . . " But she continued to stare at Philip's face and he continued to blush.

The waiter finished pouring coffee and left, not bothering to conceal his smile.

Dixie was staring at Philip still.

There was a momentary silence at the table and then Beecher Stubbs descended on them, with Calvin trailing behind.

"Well, there you *are*," she said, "just sitting right there with these Kizer people and I didn't even see you. I was telling Calvin, 'Calvin,' I said, 'have you ever known anybody to get a Chair that deserved it so much?' And Calvin, of course, corrected my grammar, but it's true, it's absolutely true, and I think you're the most adorable couple at the Hospital. I do. You are. And Calvin does too though he would never say it. You know Calvin. But everybody loves him anyway. They do, Calvin, who could help it? Well, enjoy your breakfast. Oh, you've eaten already. Well, enjoy it anyway. And you nice Kizers, you enjoy it too. Never mind us. We're just going to flit away. Come on, Calvin, we're keeping them. By-ee."

Calvin raised his hand in a vague salute and followed Beecher to the door.

Hal was about to say something, but Philip put his hand up to stop him. "Despite all that," Philip said, "Beecher Stubbs is very nice. And smart. And a good friend."

"So?"

"So don't say it."

Hal thought about this. "All right then, tell us about your Chair. What does it get you? In perks, I mean, and in hard cash?"

"That would be telling," Philip said.

Dixie was staring at him still. She had moist dark eyes, he noticed.

"A Chair's a Chair," Philip said. "It's a nice honor. But it doesn't change your life. You are who you are."

"Yes," Dixie said. "Yes, exactly!"

They all looked at her.

"You've had a lot of Chairs, have you?" Hal asked her. "Your academic experience qualifies you to pronounce on the difference a Chair makes in your life? You should have told me earlier, Dixie. I'd have made you my first wife instead of my second."

"Stop," Philip said. "Jesus!"

"Only kidding. Dixie loves it, don't you, Dix."

"I was agreeing with Philip," Dixie said. "He said, 'You are who you are,' and I was agreeing with him."

"Words to live by," Hal said. "Well, listen, sorry this got a bit rocky. I just wanted to congratulate you two with a little breakfast. No harm done, I hope." He waved at the waiter. "Gimme that bill, will you," he said, and the waiter produced it at once. Hal glanced at it, dropped two twenties and a ten on the table, and pushed back his chair.

In the parking lot, Hal shook hands with Philip and patted Maggie on the shoulder and said, "See ya," and started toward his car. "What a day! What a fabulous day!" he said loudly, and slipped his arm around Dixie's waist. They walked on for a moment, but suddenly Dixie pulled away and turned back toward Philip.

Philip had held the car door for Maggie and was coming around to the driver's side when Dixie put one hand on his arm and, fixing him with those moist dark eyes, said softly to him, "I know." And then she was gone.

"Quel breakfast!" Maggie said as Philip got into the car. Then, noticing how pale Philip looked, she said, "Let's hope we've seen the end of *them*."

TWO

5

No psychiatrist would do what he had done. Philip knew that, he knew it well, and he told himself so over and over again.

Psychiatrists were people, they were men and women, and they had the same problems and failings and virtues that other people had. But they were conscious people, they were reflective and analytical people. They did crazy things, sure, but when they did them, they asked themselves what they were doing, and why, and who was kidding whom. They didn't just pack up their brains at age forty-five and start breaking into houses.

For thirty of his forty-five years, Philip Tate had been more aware than most people that the mind plays tricks.

As a boy he had scared himself with phantoms in the night, creating intruders out of creaking floorboards, shadows on the window blinds, the terrors of sheer silence.

Later he re-created these phantoms for his little sister, making her cry, convincing her that they were all going to die. Which we are, he said coolly when he was chastised.

Later still he discovered that the brain has many other functions besides the generating of fear. He was fascinated by the thought that he was thinking, that he was thinking of himself thinking and feeling, and that everybody else could do the same thing. You just had to get there first, especially where emotions were concerned. So he had married Maggie as soon as he finished college.

As a doctor he had studied the interaction of the brain and body, as an endocrinologist he dealt with hormonal and bio-chemical mediators affecting the brain and its functions and its malfunctions, and as a psychoanalyst he explored once again the dark passages Freud had opened to the caves of anxiety and repression and unacknowledged fantasy. He had been psycho-analyzed by a Freudian and later by a Jungian and he had come to agree that everything was sexual in the broadest sense, and therefore hardly sexual at all, except sometimes. He had stud-ied Ferenczi and Rank and Reich, Judith Mitchell and Philip Rieff and Adolf Grunbaum. He had written books on Freud's Rat Man, and Jung's Shadow. He was contemplating a study of Adler.

This was the background he brought with him when he broke into the Kizers' house.

He pondered his actions, his motives, even his gestures of that night. He took notes. He analyzed the notes as if they were notes on a patient. He burned the notes. He studied case histories. He read up, yet again, on sociopathy. In the end he came to the con-clusion that he was dealing with the irrational. No explanation, no examination would yield more than that. He had done some-thing morally and legally indefensible. It was wrong. It was much more than wrong: it was in essence self-destructive.

Yet he had done it.

And he wanted to do it again.

6

It was Sunday morning and Cole was about to leave for Baltimore after his long weekend with the family. The visit had gone well despite Philip's nervousness and Maggie's reliance on pills. There were no family quarrels, no awkward moments. Best of all, the weekend was almost over.

Cole and Philip were still seated at the breakfast table. For this last morning, Maggie had made them pancakes, Cole's favorite, and sat with them while she drank a cup of coffee. They chatted about Cole's first year at med school, his grades, his summer research assistantship. Philip asked questions and Cole answered them, slowly, thoughtfully, as if Philip were his academic adviser rather than his father. They finished breakfast and the review of Cole's career at exactly the same time. Maggie excused herself and went upstairs to bathe.

Cole waited a moment and then pushed his chair away from the table and looked at his father.

"Mother's worse, isn't she," he said.

Philip raised his eyebrows and said nothing. Cole had been named for Maggie—Cole was her maiden name—and they'd always been especially close. Philip was no longer jealous of this closeness.

"What is it?" Cole asked. "What's going on?"

"Is something going on?"

"Father." Cole's voice was sad. "I'm twenty-three years old. I don't have to be told that something's going on." He waited. "She's drinking—a lot, I suspect—and her eyes have that pill-head look. And she moves like a fucking somnambulist."

"Watch your language."

"My language isn't the problem, Father."

"Do you think she's unhappy?"

Cole laughed, an ironic snort.

"Because of me, do you think? Because of our marriage?"

"Can she teach like this? Does she meet her classes? Grade papers? Does she *function*?"

"Yes. Yes, of course. But now that school is over, she doesn't have to worry about meeting classes or grading papers and she can just . . . I don't know what to do. I don't know what she wants. I . . . don't know."

"Father, look at me," Cole said. "Is it problems with sex? It's been my experience that most problems in marriage begin with problems in bed. I know it's not easy to talk about, particularly with me, but if that's the problem you'd better face it. And soon."

Philip looked at him. His own son, talking to him this way about sex. Cole barely knew about sex. He was only twenty-three and maybe he knew about fucking, but he didn't know about sex.

"Father?"

"I'm forty-five years old. I've fathered two kids. I think I'd know if there were a problem in bed, Cole."

"Would you? In your own bed? I know you'd be very helpful if the problem were the Stubbses' or the McGuinns' or the Fioris', but would you recognize problems in your own bed? It's been my experience that people who are expert with problems of other people are terrible with their own."

"That's been your experience?"

"I'm afraid so."

"And would you mind telling me exactly where all this experience comes from?"

Cole looked at him, uncomprehending. "I've had relationships," he said, "with women *and* men. I'm another, separate adult, Father. I'm not just an extension of you."

Philip, stunned, said nothing.

"And I happen to know that failure in relationships always shows up first in bed."

"Does it indeed?"

"It does."

"You sleep with women *and* men? Jesus Christ!"

"It's no big deal," Cole said. "One has to experiment."

"*One* has to. I can't believe this. I can't believe we're having this conversation."

"The point is that Mother is deeply, deeply unhappy. And I was simply asking you if there was trouble in bed. That's all. I was just asking a simple question."

"Well, there isn't. Trouble. In bed."

"All right. Fine. I was just asking."

"Jesus Christ."

"Fine. Case closed. It's just that your generation has a lot of problems with sex and booze. They seem to go together."

"That's been your experience too, has it?"

"Be defensive all you want, Father, but the fact is that Mother's got a problem you're not dealing with."

They sat in silence for a while.

"Well, she's got to see somebody. A shrink or a . . . somebody. Get her to see that new guy, Kizer."

"He's an ass."

"Get her to see McGuinn then."

"Mm."

"Promise?"

"Yes!"

Cole looked at his father for a long moment. For the first time he noticed the signs of age in his face. He looked exhausted.

"I'm glad about your Chair," Cole said.

Philip smiled at him. The Chair. A week had passed since the Chair dinner at Aspergarter's, and the break-in, and the breakfast at Town Line. He had not heard a word from Dixie Kizer or from Hal or from the police. "I know," Dixie had said, but then nothing further. No phone call. No visit. No cryptic note left in the mailbox or slipped under the door or pinned to his office bulletin board. None of the things he had feared. Maybe he had misheard what she said. Maybe none of it had ever happened at all.

"You done good, Father," Cole said.

Maggie appeared, smiling, all in white.

"C'est moi," she said, and did a pirouette, "the wife of the Goldman Chair."

Philip felt very tired.

Emma was home for an overnight visit. She had intended to stay the whole week, she explained, but the professor in charge of the dig had suddenly scheduled an orientation meeting in Los Angeles, so she would have to leave on Tuesday morning. It was a bummer, she said. It was all very complicated. The truth, however, was less complicated than appeared. For weeks now she had been sleeping with the professor in charge of the dig and he had invited her to Los Angeles for a three-day fling at Disneyland and she couldn't bear to pass it up. He was fifty years old and terrific fun. She lied only because she wasn't sure her parents were sophisticated enough to swing with it. And she didn't want to upset Mother . . . because . . . well.

Maggie took her shopping in the morning and Emma dutifully trailed her through Bonwit Teller and Neiman Marcus and

Ann Taylor until she couldn't stand it anymore and insisted they go to Eddie Bauer, where she bought a great pair of hiking boots, two pairs of jeans, and a dozen white cotton tees. They don't wear pumps on a dig, Emma explained. The tougher the shoes, the better. White tee shirts could be changed three times a day, if necessary, and jeans were perfectly proper attire for *wherever* they might eat. They were going to an island with no name. There were no restaurants. There were no houses. They would sleep in tents. She didn't need anything dressy, thank you, not anything. But then she relented and let Maggie buy her a Hermès scarf, red with a thin gold band around the edges, and suggested they have lunch at Neiman Marcus. She knew that would make Maggie happy.

"You look really good, Mother."

"For an old girl," Maggie said.

"You've got wonderful color. And you don't look tired at all."

Maggie said nothing.

"I mean . . ."

"What *do* you mean?"

The waitress came and they ordered iced tea and a salad.

"I'm really excited about this dig," Emma said. "It's a chance to really get into the field and learn something. I'm only a sand-sifter, of course, but that's how you begin, and Bubby—he's the professor in charge—Bubby thinks I've got what it takes."

"Bubby?"

"Robert Winfield is his name, but everybody calls him Bubby. He's cool." She reddened a little. "He's dreamy."

"Dreamy?"

"Handsome. And, like, really sexy."

Maggie thought for a moment and then decided to say it. "You like this man a lot? How old is he?"

"Oh Mother, he's fifty, for God's sake."

"Still."

"It's archeology I love, Mother, not men. There's nothing to worry about. It's just exciting. I mean, it's so *exciting*. Haven't you ever felt that something was so exciting that nothing else mattered?"

"Yes."

"Well then you know."

"Yes, but I married him. He's your father."

"No, I mean work. Study. Like your Ph.D."

This was something Maggie never talked about.

"Can I talk about it? Just a little? Mother?"

Maggie had been at Harvard studying for a Ph.D. in English when she married Philip and decided to drop out, just for a short while. It was a perfect time for a break. She had already passed her comps and she could continue to read toward her dissertation and she would go back as soon as Philip finished medical school. It was a temporary thing. They needed the money and she needed a rest from the Ph.D. grind: all those years spent on Jane Austen. Meanwhile she got a secretarial job. When Cole was born she put aside her work on Austen, and when Emma was born she gave up all thought of finishing the Ph.D. She had a private bonfire of her dissertation notes—nothing dramatic, just a quick afternoon fire in the back garden—and became a full-time mum. God knows, it took full time and more. Now, with the kids away at college, she taught Freshman Composition at U. Mass. Boston. They hired her, she suspected, because of Philip. Everybody knew Philip.

"Well?" Maggie said.

"Go back, Mother, and finish your degree. Harvard would take you back, and even if you never use the degree, you'd have it. It would mean something to you. It would mean—"

Beecher Stubbs descended at that moment, delighted to see Emma and pleased that Maggie looked so well—so young and so *well*—and wasn't Dixie Kizer sweet to go with her to the fat lady store when she herself was a size eight, or ten at most, but probably an eight. Dixie was a dear.

Maggie and Emma looked over at the table where Dixie sat alone. They smiled and she returned their smile.

And how wonderful, Beecher said, that Emma was going for a dig in Greece or somewhere and Cole was doing research at Hopkins, it was clear that Maggie and Philip had done something magic with those kids, she had been saying exactly that to Calvin only yesterday. She had to dash now and let them finish their salads—so health-conscious and smart of them—and she would call, she would call.

"Get the Ph.D., Mother," Emma said, "or you could turn into Beecher Stubbs. Think about it."

They ate in silence for a while and then Maggie said, "Maybe I'll look into it."

"Promise?"

"Promise. But not a word to your father."

"It'll be our secret! Terrific! Oh, I'm so excited for you, Mother, I'm gonna tell you *my* secret. I'm in a relationship with Bubby. And, Mother, he's really wonderful."

"A relationship? Oh, darling. You're only nineteen."

"Twenty, almost. And age has nothing to do with it."

"But Emma . . ."

"It's not like I'm in love with him or anything."

"Em, sweetheart . . ."

"I'm just *seeing* him, for Christ's sake." She was trying very hard to be reasonable.

"Seeing?"

"God! Bubby is right! You should never tell your parents anything!"

Maggie reached for her glass of wine. "It's just that I don't want you to get hurt," she said. "It's so easy, at your age, to make a terrible mistake."

"At my age?"

"At any age." Maggie put down the glass. "Look at *me*," she said.

On Monday Philip and Maggie drove Emma to the airport for her flight to Los Angeles. They sat in the lounge and made obligatory conversation.

"You've got your ticket? Money? A book?" Philip said. Emma nodded. Maggie said, "I hope it's a good flight. I hope you don't get stuck with somebody awful or boring. I hope there's somebody to meet you in L.A." Emma smiled and nodded again. "These places get more crowded every day," Philip said, "and yet they claim they're losing money." "I hate airports," Maggie said. They all agreed.

Finally it was over and Emma's flight was announced.

They kissed good-bye, and then they kissed again, and this time Emma leaned close to her father and whispered, "Cole is wrong. There's nothing wrong with Mother. Just try to persuade her to go back to school." Then with a big smile, she gave him another hug, and her mother another hug and a kiss, and rushed off, the last to board the flight. Maggie and Philip waited until she disappeared from sight.

Driving home, they were quiet for a long while and then Maggie mentioned, casually, that Emma was seeing her archeology professor.

"Seeing? In quotes?"

"In quotes. He's fifty years old."

"Jesus Christ. And she's nineteen."

"Twenty, almost."

"Is she all right? Is she gonna be all right? Did you talk to her?"

"What she's doing is irrational," Maggie said. "You can't talk people out of doing what's irrational."

"Are you okay?"

"I'll survive."

"Shit, we'll all *survive*."

Maggie fell silent.

Philip, driving, fell silent too. He was thinking that with almost no effort he could turn the steering wheel some few inches to the right and press his foot hard on the accelerator, doing eighty, then eighty-five, and he could crash the car into one of those huge concrete and steel overpass supports. It would take less than a minute. A fiery explosion. And it would all be over.

He lifted his foot from the accelerator and they slowed down from sixty-five to sixty and then to fifty-five.

"The life you save," Maggie said, "may be your own."

Philip looked over at her.

"It's from Flannery O'Connor," she said. "I've been thinking about going back to school."

7

Beecher Stubbs was the daughter of a psychiatrist who had raised her to believe that anything could be talked about. She was disappointed, therefore, that her lunch with Dixie Kizer had produced so little. She had hoped to sound Dixie on her friendship with Maggie Tate, and if it appeared they were close enough, to ask Dixie to intervene with Maggie about her drinking, which, it was now clear, had become a problem. Philip didn't see it, obviously, since he'd done nothing about it. And somebody had to do something. Why not Dixie? But it turned out Dixie scarcely knew Maggie and anyway she had her own troubles. Hal Kizer, Beecher suspected, was into drugs or perhaps boys, but whatever it was, she could see that poor Dixie also needed help.

"Calvin," she said, "I think you should speak to Philip. Somebody's got to intervene."

Calvin was reading the newspaper and did not reply.

"Gin," she said. "The consolation of sailors and scrubwomen. Somebody should speak to Philip."

She said, "Philip should do something."

And she said, loudly, "Calvin!"

He looked up from his newspaper.

"I'm talking to you, Calvin. Your reading is an act of aggression."

He lowered his newspaper, closed his eyes, and listened.

"I'm a friend of Maggie's, but I can't do it. She's too private. She's too, I don't know, *good* for me to confront. I'm not afraid of anybody, as you know, but . . ."

"I know."

". . . but there's something about her, she's essentially superior—I mean, she not only thinks she is but she *is* —and I can't be the one to do it."

"I think that's very wise of you."

She gave him a look.

"And then there's Dixie Kizer and that husband. She wouldn't tell me what's wrong, but I sense these things, you know, I intuit."

"What did she tell you?"

"Well, she told me about this dream she had. In this dream she was sleeping on her chaise longue—she says 'longue,' French pronunciation—and she became aware of somebody standing in the room looking at her. You know, that old dream. So she woke up and she realized, she said, that she was both terrified and in love. That's the point, Calvin. Terror and love. So it has to be the husband. I don't think he hits her, I asked her straight out and her answer was unequivocal, no. She wasn't faking it. I think it must be sex. Boys, perhaps, or couples. Yes, couples." She brightened at the thought. She stopped pacing. "Or maybe whole groups of people. Orgies. You'll have to find out, Calvin."

"Leave these people alone, Beecher. It sounds like they have quite enough trouble already."

"Well, Calvin, we have obligations as thinking people and as citizens and as members of the medical community."

Calvin put down his paper. "You're a good woman, Beecher. You're kind. You're caring. But you shouldn't meddle."

"What happened to being Christian, Calvin? Is that meddling?"

"Christianity, like everything else, has had its day. We're in the era of live and let live."

"I'll make dinner," she said. "I just can't talk to you when you're in the ironic mode, Calvin."

They looked at each other for a while.

"I'll speak to Philip," he said.

"And I'll tackle the Hal Kizer problem, whatever it is."

"Don't meddle, Beech."

She disappeared into the kitchen. She got out the milk and the bowls and the fake sugar. She opened the box of Oat Squares and put them on the table. She got two spoons.

"Dinner's ready," she called, and they set to it.

8

Two weeks had passed since "the event," as Philip had come to think of the break-in. Earlier in the week he had sat up drinking and then, on toward three o'clock, he got into his car and drove out to Winchester and swung by the Kizers' house. All the windows were dark. No sound, no movement anywhere on the street. Was she sitting in the sunroom waiting for him?

He cruised by the Aspergarters' house—why, he asked himself, why was he doing this?—and then on to the Fioris, the McGuinns, the Gaspards. He swung back again to the Kizers. How could she not have seen him that night? She must have. She had said as much. "I know," she said.

He had everything and he seemed determined to ruin it all. He was worried about his wife when really he was the one who ought to be committed. What kind of lunacy was this?

He would make one more loop down Woodlawn and then he would go home. He drove by the house, slowly. And then a second time. And a third.

Then he drove home.

9

Emma sent them ecstatic postcards from Disneyland and from Greece, and Maggie and Philip found themselves getting used to the idea that Emma, their baby, was having an affair with a fifty-year-old professor named Bubby. They didn't like it but there it was, a fact, and they had decided to live with it. Emma would grow up, she'd profit from this somehow, if only she didn't get hurt. But still, Maggie said, fifty years old? I know, I know, Philip said, it's unspeakable, it's unthinkable, and suggested that maybe, just maybe, Maggie might want to talk to a psychiatrist about Emma. He spoke cautiously, but he ended by saying that *if* she were to see a shrink, she could maybe talk about their marriage also, about whatever it was that was slowing things down between them, about . . .

Slowing things down?

Causing friction, he explained, making their relationship less smooth, coming between them sexually even. Maggie looked at him without saying anything, and so he went on. He would be willing to see the shrink too, they could make it a kind of counseling session, dueling therapies. Dual therapies, he meant. He laughed, sort of. And they say Freud is dead.

She would think about it, Maggie said.

In fact, Maggie had been seeing a shrink for some months, not regularly and not very successfully, and now that Emma had left for her long hot summer of dirt-sifting with the archeologist, Maggie determined to get her life in order. No pills. A weekly visit to Leona, her shrink, with complete honesty about everything. And a look-see at her abandoned work on the Ph.D.

Maggie cut down on the pills, even though it meant she slept fitfully and was cranky all the time and had begun to look like hell. She decided to make a clean break of it and throw the pills out: the Xanax, the Halcion, the Nembutal, everything. She was about to dump them down the toilet when the gesture struck her as melodramatic and self-indulgent, so she tossed the bottles into the wastebasket and the hell with it. To prove her sincerity, though, she went outside and emptied the wastebasket into the trash can behind the garage. Sayonara. An hour later she went out to the trash can and dug around in the mess until she had rescued the pills. She took them upstairs and hid them at the back of her lingerie drawer. She decided to take only half as many as before.

She made an appointment with Leona and kept it.

"I drink, I take pills, I'm turning into an angry bitch. And my daughter, who is a sophomore in college, is sleeping with her fifty-year-old archeology professor."

Leona listened.

"His name is Bubby."

Leona continued to listen.

"Needless to say, I'm unhappy." Maggie waited a moment and said, "My husband is a psychiatrist, as you know, so I'm familiar with the listening trick."

Leona smiled.

"Which means you'll have to say something."

"Very well," Leona said. "How much do you drink? What pills do you take? How often? How many? Are you angry at your daughter or at your husband or could it be you're angry at yourself? Where shall we begin?"

It was an exhausting session and Maggie did not keep her next appointment.

She did, however, make an appointment with the Chairman of the English Department. They had met off and on at the Memorial Hall Lecture Series and of course, the Chairman said, he knew her husband, by reputation at least, and so he was perfectly willing to have a talk with her.

"Now, what is it?" He gave her a smile he held a fraction too long and it turned into a grimace.

Maggie had prepared a little speech about her Ph.D. work on Jane Austen, her desire to pick up where she had left off, her anxiety about returning to scholarship after all this time. Now the speech struck her as whiny and stupid. Nonetheless he listened with what seemed like interest.

"And?" the Chairman said.

"I don't know theory," she said. "The new theory."

"There are books. There are some very good books."

"I was thinking of courses I might take that would catch me up. Until I get my feet under me."

"And what courses would these be?" He glanced at his watch.

"Well, I thought you—somebody—might recommend something. Do you offer courses in theory for people who need to catch up?"

"Mrs.—um—as I'm sure you know, everybody is caught up by the time they get here. Sorry. That's just a fact. And what, really, can a Ph.D. matter at your age?"

Written in the air between them, she read: Finis, The End, Sayonara.

"Well, thank you," she said, and stood up. "You've been very generous with your time."

"Please," the Chairman said, aware he had gone too far. "I'm sure there's something we can do for you. I'm sure the situation is not impossible at all. We have courses, of course we do, and there are books. I'm quite sure that the head of graduate studies can arrange . . ."

But she left, her face very red, and she vowed she would never invade English Department territory again.

That afternoon the head of graduate studies phoned her. Maggie told him she was busy, she could not talk, and she went upstairs and took an extra Xanax. When he phoned again the next morning she refused to answer. He left a long and detailed message explaining that he was *not* the Chairman, he was the head of graduate studies, and that he was sorry she had had to deal with the Chairman, who was a renowned scholar but a misogynist, and would she please come in and talk? They all felt very bad about this.

She knew that what they all felt bad about was offending the wife of a big deal at the Med School, but when the head of graduate studies called yet again, Maggie went in to see him. Within a few minutes he had arranged for her to sit in on Phoebe Ritson's survey of postmodern literary theory. They offered very few courses in the summer, but she was in luck because Phoebe Ritson would be teaching and Phoebe Ritson, he assured her, was *hot*.

Maggie attended Phoebe Ritson's first class and she tried to take notes, but the lecture was dazzling and incomprehensible and she realized she needed a lot of background study, and fast. She went to the library and dug out books by Husserl and Heidegger and Hegel. She settled down to look them over. They were philosophy, she expected that, but they were like no philosophy she had ever studied. There were no basic principles. There was no recognizable world. She was getting very nervous. She gathered up the books and took them to Withdrawals. She could concentrate better at home. She waited patiently in line, breathing deeply, thinking of waves breaking on the beach, and she was beginning to feel calmer, more in control, as she handed over the books to be scanned and returned to her. The checkout girl raised her eyebrows as she handed back the books. It was that finally, the raised eyebrows, that brought on Maggie's attack of panic.

Now, as she came down the steps from the library, her arms full of books, she wanted a Coke and a Xanax and she wanted to scream. She was too old, too out of touch, this was all a middle-aged delusion. She wanted a drink.

"Maggie," someone said, but she kept on. "Maggie?"

Despite herself Maggie turned to see who was calling her. It was that idiot, Dixie Kizer.

"I'm in a rush, Dixie."

"I know. I see that. Can I walk with you? To your car?"

Maggie put her head down and kept walking.

"You were so nice to me. I wanted to thank you."

"Well, you're welcome."

"I act like a fool sometimes, whenever I . . . you know. . . say something dumb and Hal points it out . . . I just don't know what to do so I . . ." The words trickled away into silence.

"You're perfectly fine. There's nothing the matter with you."

"Beecher Stubbs was very nice to me too. She likes me, she says. But I do act like a fool sometimes. Don't you think?"

Maggie stopped and turned on her. "Oh, for God's sake. You're young and you're beautiful and you've got a life ahead of you. Stop whining. *Do* something with it."

"Take a course, you mean. Like you."

Maggie stared at her. "A course?"

"I couldn't do that. I'd never have the courage."

"What makes you think I'm taking a course?"

"I went looking for you."

"But what makes you think . . . ?"

"All those books in your arms. Husserl."

"I am taking a course, as a matter of fact."

"Yes."

Despite her exasperation Maggie noticed that her panic had subsided. She was annoyed, angry even, but she was in charge. It felt good to be in charge. They were near Starbucks, and Maggie proposed that they get a coffee or something, maybe a Coke.

Dixie smiled and reached out to touch her, then drew back her hand. "Oh," she said, "that would be loverly. Simply loverly."

Maggie shot her a hard look. Loverly.

They had their Cokes and were seated on the patio and Maggie had managed to take her Xanax without being seen, she thought, and now she would find out what the hell was going on with Dixie Kizer.

"You were looking for me?" Maggie said.

"Yes."

"Why?"

Dixie's eyes began to fill with tears. "Philip told me you were taking a course."

"Philip?"

"Philip. Your husband."

"I *know* he's my husband. Why did he tell you I was taking a course?"

"I guess he thought I should know."

The woman was an idiot. Very slowly, Maggie said to her, "Why should you need to know that I'm taking a course?"

"Because it would give me an inspiration? Because if I took a course, it might give me self-confidence?"

It occurred to Maggie, finally, that Dixie Kizer must be one of Philip's patients. She was annoyed nonetheless; Philip had no right to be using her secrets to bolster the self-confidence of a patient, particularly one as idiotic as Dixie Kizer.

"I think you're just so lucky. Married to Philip and everything. It must be like a dream."

"Sometimes a dream, sometimes a nightmare."

"See? And you're witty about it too."

Maggie waited. The poor creature was a mess. And suddenly she felt herself opening to her, she wanted to embrace her and say, It's all right, it's all right.

"It's all right," Maggie said.

"Tell me about your course. I could *never* get a Ph.D. but I'd love to hear about it."

"There's nothing to tell," Maggie said. Reluctantly at first, but then with a degree of enthusiasm, Maggie told about her years at Harvard, the terrors of the qualifying exams, the discovery that she had a feeling for the form of the novel, particularly the Jane Austen novel. That was before they had made all those movies, of course. It all seemed so remote now. Form analysis of the kind she engaged in was no longer interesting. No longer valid, even. So she was trying to get a grip on the newest criticism, but it didn't seem to be criticism at all. It seemed to be some new form of writing that rose from philosophy . . . She felt a moment of panic.

"And I'm older, of course, too old for this," Maggie said. She reached for her Coke and discovered the glass was empty. Her hand had begun to shake.

Dixie was staring at the shaking hand. She had seen Maggie take a pill with her Coke. "You're not old," she said.

"Time to go," Maggie said, and gathered her books and left.

That night, as they watched the news, Maggie waited for an advertisement and then clicked the mute button on the remote control. "Listen," she said. "I know you can't talk about this because she's your patient, but I want to say something so please just hear me through. It took a great deal of courage for me to go and see that fool Chairman of the English Department and it took me a great deal more to actually go to class today. So I don't want you telling anybody about it. I regard it as a secret and I expect you to respect that. So please, *please* don't go telling anybody else about my private life."

Philip blushed. "I don't know what you're talking about."

"Yes you do. And I know you can't talk about it because of confidentiality, but what about confidentiality with *me*, Philip? What about *my* privacy? Suppose I can't do it and I have to drop out? Suppose I can't figure out what the hell they're talking about and I have to give up? Do you think I want everybody to know I tried to do it and couldn't? Do you have any idea what that kind of failure feels like? No, you don't, because you've never failed at anything. You just waltz from success to success, getting degrees and jobs and fucking Goldman Chairs, and being a saint to your women patients and a god to all the rest, and you don't have any idea what it's like to fail. And then you do this to *me*. The only thing I've got, the *only* thing, and it's secret and I may fail at it, it's very hard, it's impossible, and you go and tell someone about it! How could you! How could you!"

Philip leaned over to put his arm around her.

"I didn't do it," he said. "I didn't tell her."

She pulled away from him and ran upstairs to their bedroom.

Later, much later, he went up to her, fearing what he would find. She might be unconscious with pills or booze or, God help us, with both. Or she might be fighting mad, and vicious.

She was sitting in the lady chair by the window, deep into Hegel. Her forehead was creased with a frown and she did not hear him come in. He stood there watching her.

"I didn't tell her," he said.

She put her finger on the page to mark her place and, distracted, looked up at him and smiled.

"I don't know the woman," he said.

"I'm gonna get this if it kills me," she said, and went back to her book.

Philip went downstairs, pleased, and guilty.

10

It was three weeks now since the break-in and Philip was deal-ing with his guilt by writing a short essay on mood swings and manic depression. He had written three pages. It was a very trendy subject, what with all the half-assed talk about the miracle of personality changes effected by Prozac and the other mood elevators. Take a pill and, voilà, you're an extrovert. Take an-other and become a talk show host. Take three and become a movie star. The new drugs were wonderful, no doubt about it, but they operated totally within nature. They made the depres-sions less low, the manic highs less high. But they did not cre-ate a new person. They left you with all your free will intact, for good or for ill. As always you were stuck with what you were.

He read through what he had written and saw that it was bad. Ugly prose. Galumphing sentences. A cliché, which he struck out at once. He read it again, slowly, and thought for a while. Then he crumpled the pages together and tossed them into the wastebasket.

He glanced at the clock: time for a drink before bed. He went into the kitchen to pour himself a scotch.

He had left the car parked in the driveway. Nothing delib-erate about that; he just hadn't felt like putting it in the garage. Yes, yes, he knew what he'd say if a patient told him that. Still.

Maggie had been doing well in the past week. No drink to speak of. He couldn't be sure about the pills. She was sleeping lighter, of course; that was to be expected if she was truly off the booze. Some mornings she was awake before he was. Did she know about his night rides?

When Calvin Stubbs had told him to do something for Maggie, that even Beecher had noticed her drinking, Philip said yes, yes, he was doing what he could. But he was doing nothing except waiting and hoping. Going back for her Ph.D. might be the answer. He hoped.

Maggie had said nothing about school since the blowup over Dixie. She studied all the time, compulsively, and he tried to draw her out on what she was reading and how classes were going. Finally she told him he could read one of her papers, but not now, later, she'd tell him when, and in the meantime would he just stop pressuring her! Yes, he said, yes, okay.

He looked out at the car parked in the driveway. He could go for a little drive.

He finished his scotch and went upstairs. Maggie was sleeping soundly. He stood in the doorway looking at her. She was beautiful still, young enough to do anything she wanted, smart, talented, and yet she could not come out into the real world and play. She had all the instincts and angers of confirmed feminism but no self-assurance. She was one of the wounded, the damaged. Was he responsible?

Why, he wondered, had she loved him in the first place?

He knew why he had loved her. She made him laugh, she made him feel like a normal, sexy, attractive male, she made him feel he mattered. He could tell her anything, everything, and it was all right. But of course he hadn't told her everything. He hadn't told her about breaking into houses.

She was still sleeping soundly. He could go downstairs and get in the car and drive over to the Kizers and . . . and what? Look around. Flirt with disaster. Tempt the gods.

Why not, really?

Why not.

He closed the door softly behind him and made his way across the lawn to the driveway. He was at the car, key in hand, when he noticed a small dark MG across the street, parked one house down. In this neighborhood almost nobody parked on the street. Nor did he recognize the car. As he stood there looking, it seemed to him there was someone sitting behind the wheel. He walked down the driveway, slowly, and as he moved across the street toward the car, the headlights snapped on and the engine turned over and the car lurched suddenly and started up. Philip stared as it took off, weaving crazily down the street. He was still staring as the driver made a slow U-turn and drove back toward him and came to a stop. He approached the car. It was, of course, Dixie.

"Hello," he said.

She rolled down the window but she did not look at him.

"Hello," he said again, more softly.

"You must think I'm crazy," she said, still not looking.

"Are you okay?"

She turned to him then, her eyes huge, frightened.

"I'm sorry I upset you by . . . what I did," he said.

He said, "I didn't mean to. Upset you."

And he said, "I didn't know you'd be there."

She gave a sort of laugh. "I live there."

"I thought you'd be asleep."

"I never sleep."

"Well, I'm sorry."

She said nothing for a while and then she whispered something he couldn't hear.

"What?"

"I've waited. Every night since."

"No," he said. "No."

"I have."

"We'll have to talk. I'll have to explain. It's all my fault."

"You think I'm a fool, don't you?"

"No, it's my fault."

"I am though. I'm a fool for coming here like this. I'm so ashamed."

"Please," he said. "Please listen."

"I could kill myself. I should."

"Listen to me, Dixie," he said, but the sound of the engine drowned out his voice and he stood there in the middle of the street watching the MG disappear around a corner.

He went inside the house and had another drink. He thought, and thought some more, and then he went upstairs and got into bed.

"Did you go for a walk?" Maggie asked.

"Just a little one," he said, and they lay side by side for a long time before either of them fell asleep.

The moment he saw her in that car, fearful, desperate, Philip knew what he had to do. He had to put the blame where it belonged, on himself, and he had to urge Dixie to get a good therapist and tell him or her everything, and he had to act immediately. He phoned her the next morning and invited her to lunch. He was determined there would be nothing clandestine about this and so he arranged to meet her in the hospital cafeteria. If people made comments, well, let them. It was best that he say what had to be said in the most public place imaginable, with doctors and nurses and staff all around them. Her life was at stake and he would simply have to risk his own. He had brought it on himself.

Now they had finished eating—neither had eaten more than a few bites—and Philip leaned forward and made his little speech.

"This is an apology, Dixie," he said, "although I realize no apology is possible or adequate. I did something foolish and irresponsible and—there's no other word—absolutely crazy.

Crazy. I let myself into your house in the middle of the night, no, I *broke* into your house in the middle of the night for no reason on earth except some part of me wanted to do something . . . wrong. Something forbidden."

"Something criminal," she said.

"Something criminal," he said.

"I know," she said. "Sometimes I want to kill."

He stared at her.

"Why did you do it?" she asked. "Was it . . . ?"

"It was crazy," he said. "That's all, it was just crazy." They were silent for a moment. "Well, I'm sorry."

She smiled and said nothing.

And then, though he wanted not to, he asked, "Did you tell Hal? Does Hal know?"

"I thought it must be a dream," she said.

"I'm sorry."

"Hal's at a conference. In Denver."

Philip knew that.

"And yourself," he said, "are you all right?"

"I'm all right," she said.

"I mean, you struck me the other night for instance, at the Apergarters', well, as tense? Is tense the right word?"

"I don't sleep well, and sometimes I have a drink before bed to help me sleep, and . . ." She looked down and her face went pale and he wanted to reach over and touch her.

"Maybe you should talk to someone? See someone. Do you think?"

"A shrink, you mean?"

"Well, yes, or a clergyman or a doctor. But someone."

"I'm done with shrinks."

"Well, think about it."

"You're very kind," she said. "You are. Truly."

They looked at one another, embarrassed suddenly, and Philip got up. "You were good, Dixie," he said, "to come in and have lunch with me. And to listen to me fumble through an explanation. And I hope this puts the matter to rest. Okay? I hope so, at least. I feel I owe you something more than an apology, so if there's anything I can do for you, ever, you must feel free to ask." His voice went on and he half listened to it and marveled yet again at the power of the brain to be both present and absent at the same time, to produce words that expressed all the right and necessary things while pondering the question, Is this pity or love I feel and does the difference matter?

"Awfully nice seeing you," he said.

"Very nice," she said.

And they shook hands.

It was only a little after midnight when he stood outside the door and felt above the ledge for the key. He didn't need it. The door had been left unlocked. He passed through the entryway, the kitchen, the dining room. He paused. His breath caught in his throat and his heart began to beat faster. He entered the living room and moved to the piano and beyond it. Dixie was out there, lying on the wicker couch.

He stood in the doorway and looked at her. She sat up on the couch but said nothing.

He moved toward her, sat down, and kissed her lightly on the lips. She returned his kiss. They sat with their arms around one another, sad, silent. She was shaking.

"I'm not very good at this," he said.

"Neither am I," she said.

And so, incredibly, they made love.

11

Hal poured himself another cup of coffee. He had made his breakfast—scrambled eggs and sausage—and he had eaten it, rinsed the dishes, and stacked everything in the dishwasher. Now it was coffee time; time to think through his day.

Patients in the morning, three of them, each touching in his own way. First he'd see James, sexual dysfunction masquerading as manic depression. Then Edgar, whom he had seen twice and who so far had not spoken. It would be fun to get him talking finally. Then Cato, the real thing, with highs that were so wild and exhilarating he wouldn't let go of them, not even to be sane. Of course, the lows were so low that they were bound to end in suicide eventually, but try convincing Cato of that. Hal envied Cato those highs; he couldn't help it. He loved his work. If only people could accept themselves and enjoy it, there'd be a lot less misery in this world.

Lunch with the residents. They did a lot of sucking up and they made wild attempts to get his attention and hold it, but still they were good kids. He'd have to watch himself though, because he knew all that sucking up was bad for his ego. It wasn't right to trade on their need to impress. He hated to admit it, but more than once lately he'd caught himself pontificating, not an attractive quality.

Not attractive either to light out at Dixie whenever they were in public. Why did he do that? He made a mental note.

Business meetings after lunch and more futile attempts to slash the budget. A proposal to consolidate off-campus and on-campus clinics. New computing systems to replace clerical help. Oh sure, good luck. Every time they tried stuff like that, they ended up doubling the size of the staff. Then he'd have some research time—a good afternoon stretch of three or four hours—then a shower, a drink with Dixie, and the obligatory dinner at the Gaspards. Poor old Gaspard would repeat all his daughter's molestation charges and refute them one by one and then start all over again. He'd ask for advice and not listen. He'd ramble and denounce and drink. And then they'd all be able to go home.

And then. And then. Off to Boston for a sex seminar with Theda. Do me, do me, like you done done done before. If only Dixie could realize this wasn't just kinky; it was serious stuff; it was taking him somewhere important. It could be sweeter than anything she ever imagined. Sweet.

Inspired, he rinsed his coffee cup and put it in the dish-washer. He went to the cabinet, took down the jar of maple syrup, and dipped his index finger in it. He went upstairs to Dixie. He'd show her how sweet.

She was sleeping with her face turned toward the door. He approached the bed, and with his left hand he pulled the sheet down from her shoulders. Lightly, carefully, he lowered the strap of her nightgown until her right breast was exposed. It was per-fect, beautifully shaped, with great tone. She was, in looks at least, a really sexy woman. He rubbed the maple syrup on the exposed nipple, making circles, tracing the lines and ridges, slowly. Dixie opened her eyes and looked at him. He smiled at her. She was startled, but she did not move. She watched what he was doing. He lowered his face to her breast, lapped at the nipple, softly, then eagerly. He looked up at her and smiled. "Sweet?" he asked. He lapped the nipple and then he grazed it with his teeth, lightly, a puppy nip, and lapped it again. He bit down, just a little, barely at all, and he was going with the moment, he was hard now, it was good now, and it was going to get better. Another little bite. And then she ruined everything. She screamed and tried to push him away. She began to cry.

He lifted his head and stood looking down on her. He forced a smile.

"You'd get to like it," he said, "if you'd just let yourself go." She covered her face.

He took her hands away and kissed her softly on the mouth. "I've made you coffee," he said. "Enjoy."

Philip was having lunch again with Dixie Kizer. They were in the hospital cafeteria and, though they had been there for more than a half hour, they had not yet been able to exchange a private word. People kept pausing at the table to say hello or to ask some dumb question or, it would seem, to engage in chat with the sole purpose of preventing a serious conversation.

To each of them Philip dutifully introduced her. "This is Dixie Kizer, a friend." And when they stayed longer, he would add, "Dixie is married to Hal Kizer. We're having lunch." So everybody knew who they were and what they were doing.

Finally they were left alone.

"How are you, Dixie?" Philip's voice was intimate.

"I'm all right," she said. "I'm fine."

"I am very *very* sorry. I can never forgive myself for doing that . . . you know. But I *am* sorry. My only concern right now is you. Are you all right?"

"Yes," she said.

"Of course you're all right. What I mean to say is that I never meant to upset you. I mean, this can never happen again and it should never have happened in the first place. I know that. *You* know that. Above all, I don't want to do you any injury. Do you understand?"

"I'm a fool," she said.

"Please. *Please* don't say that, Dixie. I'm the one who's the fool."

"I love you," she said.

"Don't say that. Please don't *feel* that. It's all wrong. And it's all my fault."

"You're so kind. You're so gentle."

"I'm not. I try to be, but as you see, I fuck up. Excuse the language. I'm worried, I'm very worried."

"I know you are. But I'm not. I'm fine."

"This can't happen again."

"No?"

"It just can't."

"Your wife is kind too. I followed her and I talked to her. We talked about her studies."

"And how did you know about her studies?"

"I followed her. To class."

"Dixie."

He looked at her, unable for the moment to comprehend.

"Sometimes I follow people."

"You can't do this," he said. "Poor Maggie."

"Is she angry with me?" She thought for a moment. "Is she angry with you?"

This was insane. And he had brought it on himself.

"Is she smart, smart, smart? I bet she is."

Philip thought of Maggie this morning as he had last seen her. She was already out of bed by the time he woke up, and when he went downstairs to breakfast, he found her bent over the table with books spread out all around her. Her face was strained with concentration and she was picking at the knuckles of her left hand. "Good morning," he had whispered, and set about making coffee. "I'll never get this stuff," she said, and she did not look up until he was about to leave. "Bye," he said, and gave her a kiss. "I'm so frightened," she said. He had kissed her again, and left.

"Maggie works very hard," he said. And, though he had not intended to, he added, "She thinks you're my patient. I didn't say you weren't."

"I'd like to be. Your patient."

"I can't, Dixie. You can't."

"I'd like to be anything of yours."

A busboy came and said, "You through?" and started piling their dishes. Philip waited in silence, but Dixie repeated, "I'd like to be anything of yours."

The busboy looked up at her and then at Philip.

"I'm sorry," she said.

"We've got to be sensible," Philip said. "You're not in love with me, Dixie, and I'm not in love with you." She looked away, hurt. "It's just something that happened. We made love and we shouldn't have. We both have wives—marriage partners, I mean—and what we've done is, quite simply, adultery. And we can't do that. We're more responsible than that. Aren't we." It was not a question. "We are. You know we are."

"If that's what you want," she said.

"It's not a question of what I want, it's a question of what's got to be. I think this is the last time we can see each other, Dixie. Can we agree to that? We just have to put all this behind us."

"If you say so."

"But I'm right, am I not?"

"I guess."

"So that's settled," he said. "And you will—promise me— you will talk this over with a good psychiatrist. Someone you trust. Someone who cares about you. Agreed?"

"I guess."

"Thank you," he said, and surprised himself by adding, "I'll pray for you."

She smiled, a little sad.

"That's it, then."

"But we can still be friends, can't we? We can still have lunch? Sometimes?"

This was impossible. She simply did not get it.

"Philip?"

"No. I'm sorry. This is it. It's done."

He wondered what would come next. He feared she would cry or get hysterical or start shouting things, but she merely smoothed the back of her left hand with her right, adjusted her ring, and finally reached for her handbag.

"I understand," she said, "and of course you're right."

She stood and shook hands with him, smiling, and then she left.

Maggie had still not dressed. She had spent the entire morning, in her caftan and slippers, trying to make sense out of Husserl's "phenomenological reduction." Husserl seemed to her an awful lot like Descartes and she didn't see how the study of pure phenomena would lead her anywhere in the neighborhood of literature. Husserl wanted scientific certainty, which was very nice, she supposed, but the whole point of literature was that it dealt *not* with certainty but with mystery. Nevertheless she made an act of faith and went on studying: "deep structures," "transcendental modes of inquiry," "eidetic abstraction." She wanted to cry.

At lunchtime she ate a peanut butter sandwich and drank a glass of milk. She hated milk and she hated peanut butter, but she needed the protein and the energy and, let's face it, the distraction. The truth was that she needed a Xanax, but she was not going to give in. Not now. She was going to conquer Husserl and hermeneutics and reception theory, and she was going to progress to structuralism and semiotics and all the rest of it, and she was eventually going to finish her goddam Ph.D.

She took two aspirins for her headache and bent over her books once again.

* * *

Beecher Stubbs had phoned Hal Kizer's office at five of nine to ask for an appointment at one. Nothing urgent, she said. Seeing her at one would mean missing a budget meeting, so Hal said yes, come ahead. Besides, she was up to something and it would be interesting to find out what.

It was Beecher Stubbs's good luck to pass by the hospital cafeteria while Philip Tate and Dixie Kizer were having lunch and it was her further good luck to notice they were deep in what seemed an intimate conversation. Luck had never been a problem for her. She had, after all, married Calvin. If she were the kind of person who bought lottery tickets, Beecher had no doubt she would win.

She arrived in his waiting room just as Hal Kizer opened the office door to usher her inside.

"It's personal, of course," she said, "but then it would be, wouldn't it, or I wouldn't be talking to a shrink. It's about sex," she said.

Hal Kizer looked at her and said nothing. Sex? At her age? In her shape?

"You're probably thinking, sex, at my age? And I wouldn't blame you, because I'm no spring chicken. But sex is never a problem, is it, so long as it's working well. In that respect, it's like money. If you've got it, you never think about it. It's only when you don't have it that it becomes a problem." She paused. "Am I talking too much? Would you like to interrupt and say something?"

"Tell me about yourself," he said.

"I'm talking about sex that's a leetle teeny tiny bit off the beaten path," she said. "Not rough sex, as I think they call it, with manacles and everything, but sex that has a little spice to it, or vinegar maybe, the kind that makes you look up and take notice."

"Tell me about *you*," he said. "Tell me about growing up and what you wanted to be and what you feared to be and then what you are. Or what you think you are."

"All that?" she said, and filled nearly the whole hour.

She was a psychiatrist's daughter, like nearly everybody, and she had majored in psych at college. Radcliffe. She had married Calvin straight out of school because he was adorable and because he didn't mind that she was plump going on fat and because he said he loved her. And it turned out he did love her; imagine that. They had raised three lovely boys—Calvin Jr., Wesley, and Luther—who were doctors but not shrinks. Her hobbies were growing roses and parapsychology and she felt there was a connection between them because she had all of her most astonishing revelations about people while pruning the roses. Pruning, hmm, what do you make of that? Which brought her back to the issue of sex. How did he feel about sexual variation? Combination? Kinky stuff?

He smiled. "And why are you asking me this?"

"You're a psychiatrist and I'd like to know what you think? I'm seeking help?"

"For yourself? I don't think so."

She found it very hard not to tell the truth so she said nothing.

He looked at her, amused. She was smart. She was probably, as he had thought from the first, a troublemaker.

She continued to look at him.

"You're very interesting," he said.

"Pshaw."

"So what do you want, really?"

"I'm testing my instincts."

"About yourself? Or about me?"

"About you," she said, "because I worry about Dixie."

"Dixie has nothing to fear from me, if that's what you mean."

"That is what I mean."

"Though she has plenty to fear from herself."

Beecher thought for a moment. This was true, she had known this from the start, but did he mean what she meant or something altogether different? Had her instincts misled her?

"Time's up," he said. "I think this will be it, don't you? No further appointments."

"One more," she said. "A follow-up."

He escorted her to the door.

"We'll see," he said.

He had been tempted, just for laughs, to tell her about his seminar tonight with Theda, but he knew that, given the circumstances, she would not find it a laughing matter.

It was going to be a long night, a difficult night, and so Philip had come home early to spend some time with Maggie.

"Do you want to go shopping?" he said. "Get you a new dress for the dinner tonight? Something terrific?"

Maggie looked from Philip to her books and then again to Philip.

"I have to work," she said. "I have to *get* this goddam stuff."

"Maybe a break would help." He put his hand on her shoulder and, bending over, kissed her. "A coffee break?"

She shook her head.

"Okay. How about if I just get a book and sit with you? At this end of the table."

"No!" she said.

"I'll go shower. Do good, sweetheart."

Maggie continued to read Husserl's *The Idea of Phenomenology*. She heard him go upstairs and turn on the shower and she listened for a moment to the rush of the water. She read and she read. After a long time she became aware that there was no longer the sound of water, there was only the ticking of the kitchen clock and the beating of her heart and the terrible pulsing in her brain. And she was still on the same page. Well, she *would* get it. She would not let Husserl defeat her. And she would not take a pill either.

A moment later she lowered her head to her book and, soundlessly, began to cry.

The dinner party was exactly what they all expected. Old Gaspard had rounded up the usual suspects—Aspergarters, Tates, McGuinns, Fioris, the redoubtable Leona Spitzer, and a new addition, the Kizers—and the text for the evening was recovered memory. The subtext, of course, was that any and all of them might expect to be asked to testify on behalf of Gaspard. And they'd better be ready: what was happening was madness, the accuser was believed automatically, no matter how preposterous the accusation, anarchy was loosed upon the thinking world.

His own case, for instance, Gaspard said. Was there ever a better father or mother than him and Mrs. G? No, there was not. Was there ever a more loved and protected daughter than their Colette? No, there was not. This whole lawsuit business was the fault of Colette's psychiatrist, a crazy woman from southern California, who went around sowing ideas in the minds of unhappy, unattractive young women that they must have been molested in their childhood and that's why their lives were all screwed up now. What were her credentials anyhow? She'd been to some touchy-feely institute in Los Angeles, and she'd worked with kids who really had been abused by their parents, there was proof of that, and now she thought every woman who was forty and depressed and devoid of self-esteem must have been molested as a child. It was irresponsible. It was lunatic. He was an eminent psychiatrist and he was being sued by his own daughter. Had anybody ever heard of anything so crazy?

No. Nobody had. And it was too sad to talk about. None-theless, for longer than they wanted to, they talked about it. Then the dinner had to be served and, mercifully, Gaspard was called out to do the wine. They had a hired girl—Goldie, age seventy—who helped Mrs. G get dinner on the table but Gaspard allowed nobody but himself to do the wine. With apologies, he left the guests to their own company.

Conversation picked up at once. They talked about the bud-get cuts that were killing the Med School, the new and attrac-tive group of interns, the likely candidates for Dean.

"My bet is on you," Leona Spitzer said to Philip. "First the Chair, then the Deanery. It makes sense."

"I am unworthy, Lord," Philip said.

"I'll take bets," Hal said. "Listen, Phil, there's something I want to ask you about," and he put his arm across Philip's shoul-der and turned him away from the group. Within seconds, Hal had him engaged in private conversation. The others pretended not to notice.

"I didn't know you'd be here," Dixie said to Maggie. "I'm glad." She seemed very nervous.

"You look awfully nice," Maggie said. "White is so good on you, with that dark hair and those beautiful eyes."

"Oh, it's . . . well . . . you're always so kind to me." Dixie glanced over at Philip and Hal, anxious. "Your course," she said, "how is it going? Philip told me I shouldn't have mentioned that I knew about the course, but I keep thinking of you coming out of the library with all those books in your arms. Husserl."

Maggie chose not to hear the comment about Philip. "Don't mention Husserl," she said. "He's driving me out of my mind. Have you read him?"

"Oh, I haven't read anything. I was in art history."

"Stick with art history. Trust me."

"Husserl?" Aspergarter asked. "You're reading Husserl?"

"Who's reading Husserl?" Leona Spitzer asked. "Nobody reads Husserl anymore."

"She is, Maggie is," Dixie said.

"Oh, sorry," Leona said.

"She knows everything about Husserl," Dixie said.

There was a pause, a moment of silence, and someone said, softly, "You mean she's never *read* Husserl?" and there was something like contempt in the voice. Maggie had no idea who said it.

"Dinner, everybody," Gaspard called. "Please, please, before the soup gets warm."

They moved into the dining room, where they discovered the soup comment was not really a joke, since the soup was gazpacho, handsomely iced in silver bowls. Hal Kizer made oohing noises that were appreciation and satire all at once. Roberto Fiori laughed. "Num, num, num," Hal said.

Maggie was seated next to Hal, Philip next to Dixie. Hal said something to Maggie, but she didn't hear what he said. She was still hearing, "You mean she's never *read* Husserl?" and she could feel the contempt in the voice. A man's voice? A woman's? She was not sure.

Hal repeated what he had said, and again Maggie did not hear him, but it didn't matter because Gaspard was clinking his glass with a spoon, signaling a toast.

"To Philip Tate, first of all, our new Tyler P. Goldman Professor of Psychiatry, and then to his lovely wife Maggie, and we must not forget . . . ," and he went off into a speech that celebrated Chair holders old and new, forgotten and not forgotten, and eventually they were allowed to drink. Maggie listened and heard only, "never *read* Husserl?" and raised her glass and sipped her wine. Chardonnay, of course, the necessary wine this year. She sipped it again. And again.

She smiled at Philip, she entered the conversation to nod, to agree. No, she had no opinions on recovered memory. Yes, she was sure a great deal of damage was done, innocently, sincerely. And all the while she thought, Yes, I am a fake, I am a dilettante, I have never read Husserl, I can't even understand Hussserl, I can't understand anything. She looked over at Philip, who was watching her, and deliberately she reached for her glass of wine and drank. She hated him and his concern for her. His pity. She smiled at Hal and put her hand on his wrist. She asked him something and he answered—she had already forgotten what she asked—and he went on talking about manic depression as if it mattered to anybody other than the doctor and the patient. She nodded and played with her glass and said yes, she supposed it was all very complex. She sipped her wine, slowly, then again. Philip was not talking to Dixie, she noticed. In fact he seemed to be avoiding her. He was arguing with Roberto Fiori, a friendly argument with laughter on both sides, and he kept his eye on Maggie while poor Dixie was left in silence, listening to whatever she could pick up from conversations on either side of her. Maggie emptied her glass of wine.

"Poor Dixie," Maggie said across the table. "You should have some wine." Her speech was slightly slurred. "You look so pretty," she said, "in virginal white."

Dixie looked at her.

Philip said nothing, but continued to stare at Maggie. Hal too turned toward Maggie, interested in what might happen next.

"Philip is frowning," Maggie said. "Philip doesn't approve of my conversation."

"Oh," Hal said, "is Philip uptight about the word 'virgin'? Or is it something else?"

In their private little conversation before dinner, Hal had asked Philip, frankly, man to man, how he felt about sex, about—in fact—rough sex? No? Not even academically? No. Period. It has a spiritual quotient, Hal said, it's not what you think, I could explain. Not interested, Philip said. Hal raised his left eyebrow and laughed. Now, as he waited for Philip to respond, Hal again raised his left eyebrow, ready to laugh or mock or, Philip realized, to say absolutely anything, no matter how embarrassing, no matter how obscene.

"Well?" Hal said.

Philip shook his head and said nothing.

"Not a word to say? Were you this taciturn at lunch with my virginal wife?" Hal stared at Philip, smiling.

Philip glanced over at Dixie and then turned back to Hal. Maggie looked from Philip to Hal and then to Dixie.

"My secretary saw you together. A clever girl, that."

Nobody could speak. The others at table waited for something terrible to happen. There was only silence.

"More wine," old Gaspard said, "that's what we need."

"More wine," Maggie said, "exactly. Do you know that poem?

> *I hail the fool divine,*
> *Who first discovered wine.*
> *Like Leda he knew*
> *Exactly what to do*
> *In case of assault by a swan:*
> *Hang on!"*

She recited it well, with a nice pause after 'swan' and a bravura delivery of the last line. Everybody laughed, even Philip.

"I'll have some wine," Dixie said suddenly.

"*We* must have lunch, you and I," Hal said to Maggie, "since everybody's doing it. You can recite poems to me."

"I *will* have some wine," Dixie said, and gave Hal a defiant look.

"Don't look at me," Hal said, "I don't care what you drink. Who knows—it might even help." And to Maggie he said, "Tomorrow? For lunch?"

"Maybe. Maybe not."

"I'll call you," Hal said.

"This is an excellent wine, I think," old Gaspard said. "I got it at Bottoms Up. It's nine ninety-nine the bottle and a very drinkable chardonnay. I've had good chardonnays and I've had excellent chardonnays, and in the end, you know, the distinction lies primarily in the palate."

"In case of assault by a swan," Hal said, "Hang on."

"I think this is a good chardonnay," Roberto Fiori said. "I wouldn't call it an excellent chardonnay."

"I think it's excellent," Maggie said.

"I don't agree," Roberto said, and they all began to relax a little as the discussion moved inevitably in the direction of wines they had known and loved. They talked and they talked and all the while they drank the good-to-excellent chardonnay.

Philip and Maggie did not talk on the drive home. Maggie had drunk a great deal too much and she had passed through her exhilarated phase to a moment of sheer giddiness and now she was muddy and lethargic, vaguely offended at something to do with Husserl and eager for a pill that would let her go unconscious.

Philip was angry and worried and a little drunk as well. He could not make sense of what had happened at dinner. It was a hopeless muddle, a series of hostile exchanges between him and Hal Kizer, between Hal and Dixie, Dixie and Maggie, Maggie and himself. It had simply happened. It had blown up out of nowhere. They were chatting at table and suddenly, like a Pinter play, all civility was peeled away and naked, poisonous aggression was laid out on the table. A four-way assassination.

Well, he was done with this madness. Altogether done. He would salvage whatever he could of his marriage, his sanity, his fucking life. Right now what mattered to him was his wife. He would care for her. He would love her back to health. He would recapture those days before the goddam Goldman Chair, when he and Maggie were content merely to have everything. He'd do it. He would. Consider it done.

They reached home and he helped Maggie up to bed and tucked her in.

"Good night, sweetheart," he whispered.

She took his hand and crushed it against her breast. She seemed fully aware now. She began to cry, softly at first and then with loud racking sobs as if she might never stop. He sat on the bed and held her and after a long while she stopped.

"Okay?" he said. "Are you okay now?"

"I'm okay," she said, and turned her face to the pillow.

"Can I get you anything?"

"I'll sleep now," she said, and closed her eyes. When he left her and went downstairs, she got up and took a couple Xanax. She stood before the mirror looking at the wreckage. "You've never even read Husserl," she said, her mouth twisted in disgust.

"I'll be going to Boston," Hal said as he pulled into the driveway.

"So go," Dixie said.

"I've gotta change," he said. "I like loose clothes for the trip back."

"You're sick," she said.

"I'm sick? *I'm* sick? I'm not the one having secret lunches with Phil Tate. So what's the story? Are you seeing him?"

"Seeing him?"

"As a patient?"

"Maybe I'm seeing him sexually. Have you ever thought of that?"

"My little titmouse? I don't think so." He thought for a moment. "What did you tell him about me?"

"Nothing."

"But you told Beecher Stubbs something. What? Everything?"

"Almost nothing."

"Not that I care, really." He thought for a moment. "And it doesn't matter what you tell Phil Tate, you know, because I've already told him myself. You don't believe me? Tonight, before dinner, I took him aside and I asked him. He says he's not interested, but I don't believe it. I think he's like you and just afraid to let go. Look at his mouth sometime. It's wide. And just enough of it. The mouth is the giveaway. You've got the same mouth."

They were sitting in the car and he was looking at her.

"You're beautiful," he said, and slid his hand up her thigh and rubbed his thumb against her crotch. "You could come with me. Theda would love it. Live a little."

"You disgust me," she said, and got out of the car.

Hal followed her inside, showered, and changed his clothes. He put on a gray sweat suit he kept for jogging and for the sex seminars. He pushed his pelvis hard against the bureau. What an interesting phenomenon: pain that is pleasure. Just think of it. Dixie didn't know what she was missing. When he was ready to leave, he leaned into the sunroom and said, "Sure you don't want to come?"

By way of answer Dixie turned up the volume on the TV.

And so he was on Route 93 to Boston, dressed for the occasion, feeling fit and fuckish. And why not? He was a young man in his prime, a good doctor, a good psychiatrist with a rich and beautiful wife and a sincere interest in getting to the bottom of who he was. He was committed to this: finding ecstasy and finding himself within it. It was what the medieval mystics were after, and some of them had actually clued into it, whether or not they understood what they were really up to. Constance, for instance, or whatever her name was—a saint, fifteen or sixteen century—anyway, she lived on almost no food at all and drank no water and she washed the floor of her cell with her tongue. Your tongue, Constance? And did it feel good? All that dirt and shit on the floor? And how does this feel, Constance? He'd like to put his whole fist up inside her, lift her off the floor, and then toss her onto the bed. He'd lick the blood off her. He'd pry her open. He'd invent new ways to surprise her. And she'd love it.

It was ecstasy, that's what they were after. Everybody was. Nirvana. Heaven. The ultimate.

"We can't do this," Philip said. "You know that."

Dixie had telephoned and said she needed to see him.

Philip had been standing over the phone half expecting it to ring, and when it did ring, he snatched it up at once. He laughed nervously. In a movie, he thought, this would be the moment at which everything turns fatal. But this wasn't a movie.

"He's gone again, to the city," she said, and when Philip didn't reply, she added, "and he struck me."

"Struck you?"

There was silence on the line.

"What do you mean, struck you? Physically? He hit you?"

"He always does," she said. "Always."

Philip was all business now. "You should report this at once," he said. "To the police. Call the police right now and make a formal complaint."

Silence again.

"Do you hear me, Dixie?"

"I need to talk to you."

"You need to talk to the police. Tell me you'll do it. You'll call them."

He could hear her breathing.

"Dixie?"

"He didn't hit me."

Now Philip was silent.

"He hurt me, but he didn't really hit me."

He remained silent.

"I lied. Are you angry with me?"

"I thought we straightened this out at lunch, Dixie. What we did was wrong. What *I* did was wrong. I've got a wife and family and you've got a husband and we can't cause other people—"

"I'm going to take pills," she said, interrupting him. "I'm going to take too many pills."

He waited and she waited.

"I can't be part of this," he said. "I won't be."

"It's your fault. You can go to hell." She slammed down the phone.

A half hour later Philip drove by the Kizers' house to see if everything looked all right. He didn't know what he expected to see. No lights were on, but what did that mean? She might have taken an overdose of something, she might have slit her wrists, she might have just gone to bed to sleep it off. His first thought had been to notify the police, and he thought of the police once again, but what could he say to them? Maybe she's taken pills, but maybe she's just sleeping, and wouldn't you like to break down the door and find out?

He parked the car and went around to the back. The key was on the ledge. He let himself in and went to the sunroom.

"I knew you'd come," she said.

He sat down in a wicker chair a little distance from her.

"I knew it," she said. "I knew it." She knelt at his feet and pressed her head against his chest. She began to cry.

He let her finish crying and then he held her away from him. "Get up, Dixie. Come. Come." He led her to the chaise longue, where she sat down and made room for him, but he returned to his chair. He sat forward, his elbows on his knees, his face in his hands.

"Are you angry?" she said. "Why are you angry?"

He took his hands away from his face and looked at her.

"You've got to listen to me," he said. "We talked today at lunch about what happened between us. Right?"

"Yes."

"And we agreed that what we had done was reckless and destructive and that it could not happen again. It must *never* happen again. Right?"

"Yes, but you're here now."

"And I urged you to see somebody. To get some counseling."

"But I had to see you."

"Let me finish. I urged you to talk this over with a psychiatrist. Not with *me*—because I'm part of the problem—but with somebody you trust and like and who cares about you."

"Yes, yes, but—"

"No, listen. *Therefore,* cruel as it may sound, you can't call me up and say Hal has struck you or that you're going to take an overdose of pills. That's a cry for help, but you're crying to the wrong person. I can do nothing for you—I've made that impossible and you've made that impossible—and you've got to go to somebody who *can* help. You need to talk to a therapist about your unhappiness and what went on between us and whatever is going on between you and Hal. But you can't talk to me about it. I'm useless to you. I'm worse than useless."

"But I love you."

"No you don't. And I don't. And this is the really hard part, so please listen. If you call me and threaten suicide, I'll do the thing I *have* to do—professionally, morally—I will *have* to. I'll call the police and ask them to send an ambulance. And I won't come. I can't."

"You're like all of them. You're cruel. You're like Hal, only worse. At least he doesn't pretend to love me."

"I have to go." He stood, but before he could take even one step she was on her knees before him, her face pressed against his crotch, and she was saying, "Please, oh please, I'll let you do anything you want to me, you can hurt me if you want, you can—"

He pulled back from her, lifted her to her feet, and sat her again on the chaise longue. "Stop," he said. "Stop it." He held her there, away from him, his hands on her arms. "I have to go," he said, and his voice was very cold.

He left quickly, without looking back.

Hal Kizer ached all over, but particularly between his legs. Theda had tied him up with a rough hemp rope, around his ankles first, with his legs spread a good three feet apart, and then around his genitals and up tight through his ass and around his waist and then out to his wrists, also spread a good three feet apart. It was a kind of Sadean improvisation he had thought up himself; any struggle whatsoever, any movement of arms or legs simply tightened the rope around his balls, roughly, hairily, and made him harder and hungrier. And then she played with the knife, there, and there, and that magic spot just under his balls. She wouldn't cut him, even though he asked her to, not even a little. Just a nice loose play with the knife, tickle, tickle, and he writhed and the rope cut into him and he could feel his brain tumble over into blackness. In the end he nearly went unconscious. He felt himself teetering there on the edge of something black and then a blinding flash and another and then he came. It was heaven.

As he drove along 93, the stars bright and the night air cool, he put his hand, tenderly, to his crotch. The skin was raw there and felt good. How he loved this: he was exploring the limits of sexual endurance, finding the point beyond which there was nowhere to go.

Dixie could be in on this if only she would let herself go. So could Philip Tate. He let his mind dwell on Philip Tate. Was he attracted to Philip, sexually? Interesting, enigmatic Philip

Tate. The next Dean of the Medical School, no doubt. Unless, of course, that wife sabotaged him. With drink. Or pills. They all had their dirty little secrets. And what secret was *he* hiding, the decorous Philip, the wonder boy?

He turned on to West Border Road. He was almost home.

Perhaps because Philip was on his mind, Hal Kizer thought for a moment that Philip was the driver of the car that pulled out of Woodlawn as he pulled in. It was a car like Philip's and the maniac behind the wheel was doing fifty at least, but Philip was not the type for midnight rides. Philip was tucked up in bed, no doubt, with his uptight wife, thinking pious thoughts about marriage and children and the joys of the Deanery.

Hal pulled into the drive and sat there for a moment, resting. It had been a long day, but a good one.

THREE

12

Philip had resolved not to tell Maggie about his one-night fling with Dixie Kizer—he knew that telling her would be foolish, he knew it would ruin everything—but he did tell her, and afterward there was fierce silence between them.

It happened this way. Maggie had written a short paper on Robert Frost's "Mending Wall," a structural analysis in which she demonstrated that meaning in the poem was not Frost's nor the reader's but the product of shared systems of signification. She was not happy with the paper because she felt it was mere logic-chopping that produced nothing new or vital about the poem. She rethought it and rewrote it. And rewrote it a third time. Finally she gave it to Philip for his criticism. Reluctantly, he read it. He confessed he didn't understand a word of it but told Maggie to hand it in anyway and see what the hot professor had to say. So she did. Phoebe Ritson had reservations about Maggie's argument—it smacked just a little of Wellek and Warren—and she made suggestions for a substantial revision, but she nonetheless gave the paper a grade of A minus. Maggie was jubilant and to celebrate she and Philip went out to a splendid dinner. They had a bottle of good merlot, and that night they made love, and they slept—for the first time in a long time—in one another's arms. In the morning, at breakfast, Philip confessed he had slept with Dixie Kizer. He assured Maggie it had happened only once, that he and Dixie were both drunk, that it had never been repeated. "Don't say anything more," Maggie said. "I have to think what this means. For me. And for us." He was sorry, he begged her forgiveness, she must understand that it meant nothing, nothing. "To you, it means nothing. But to me?" He said he was sorry. "And to Dixie?" He said again he was sorry. Again he begged her forgiveness. He knew it would take time. "It will take more than time," she said. "It will take a whole new relationship. If I *am* able to forgive you. If I *do* decide to stay with you." That's when the silence began.

As days passed and she thought about the affair, Maggie was surprised to find it upset her less than she would have expected. He had been unfaithful. He had betrayed her. She told herself he had lied and cheated and she hated him, but she recognized her indignation as melodrama. She knew he loved her. She knew he was shattered by what he had done. She knew, since he had promised, that he would never do it again. Philip was a very simple man, really. But she was silent and let him stew.

She felt twinges of some new emotion that made her happy and then later made her uncomfortable. She had never experienced power of this kind before, and she rather enjoyed it. She had been wronged. She had been treated unjustly. She could forgive or not forgive. She could condemn him to . . . what? . . . outer darkness? Well, eventually she would forgive him, but not just yet.

Meanwhile Dixie Kizer seemed to appear in her life with increasing frequency. She was in the library, in the parking lot, at the cafeteria having coffee. At first Maggie was infuriated. That adulteress, she thought, that husband-stealer, that bitch, daring to follow me around. But after a while, Dixie seemed to her merely pitiful. And there was something peculiarly satisfying in chatting about the weather with somebody you knew had slept with your husband, but who didn't know you knew. It gave you the chance to double-think them all the time—a shrink's satisfaction, she supposed—to know the implications of what they were saying, their motives, their secret desires, and they had no idea you knew. Another kind of power. Maggie disliked herself for enjoying it, but who wouldn't enjoy it, and besides, she was the injured party, not Dixie. Dixie was just dumb. Beautiful and rich, but dumb. And not even sexy.

"How rich *are* you?" she asked Dixie one day as they walked from the library to the cafeteria. They had met for coffee nearly every day that week.

"Rich?"

"People talk all the time. They talk about me and Philip"— she paused here and looked over at Dixie—"and of course they talk about you and Hal. *You've* got the money, they say. Do you? Lots?"

"I was brought up to think it was vulgar to talk about money."

"It is. I'm vulgar. Tell me about it."

Dixie told her that she had a trust fund, two trust funds actually—one from her grandmother and one from her father—and she couldn't touch the principal but there was quite a lot of interest.

"Good," Maggie said. "Good for you. Now that wasn't so hard, was it."

The more she talked with Dixie, the more Maggie felt she could forgive Philip. There was nothing, surely, he could find attractive or interesting about this woman.

Maggie's silences became less long, less angry. She and Philip began to chat at breakfast. They went out for dinner again. They even had a cookout and invited the whole psychiatry gang. Beecher Stubbs and Calvin came, and Beecher whispered to Maggie that she was sure Philip was first choice for the Deanship, and Maggie smiled and said terrific. But when Calvin, later in the evening, told her the same thing, Maggie began to think it might really be so. Good for Philip. Good for poor old unfaithful Philip. That night they made love, tentatively, but it meant they were friends again.

Classes were not going well, however, and Maggie was studying longer and longer hours with less to show for it. Her paper on Frost turned out to have been a fluke; it was, so the hot Phoebe suggested, the product of too much Wellek and Warren and too little Saussure and Jonathan Culler. Revising it proved impossible and, discouraged, Maggie decided to write off Structuralism as one of the great lost mysteries. She moved on to Deconstruction and her confidence fell further. She began taking Xanax again, not to sleep, just to relax a little as she forced her way through Derrida and Foucault and Lacan. She couldn't understand what any of them did when they deconstructed and she couldn't figure out why they bothered. Their conclusions—that things were not what they seemed—were always relative and subjective. Nothing meant anything. Everything meant nothing. She despaired of the theory business altogether. Theory was merely a rival literature, a way of being important in the academic world even if you couldn't write a novel or a poem or a play. She wrote up these opinions as notes toward her final paper. They were stupid, she knew. They were old-fashioned. They might even be proof that she was not equipped to go back for her Ph.D. She sipped a long scotch each night while she studied. Sometimes she'd have a second. She needed it. Philip, who noticed, didn't dare say a word.

"If you've got your own money, why don't you just leave him?"

She was having coffee with Dixie and once again Dixie was whining about how she had nothing, how she *was* nothing, how greatly she envied Maggie her marriage and her family.

"But you've got your own money," Maggie said.

"Yes, but it's only money."

"Marriage is only marriage, for that matter. Do something."

Dixie toyed with her coffee cup and searched for some response.

"Do you drink?"

Dixie was startled.

"I'm playing shrink, I guess, and I don't mean to offend you, Dixie, but you seem so unhappy and you seem to have so little cause to be unhappy that I can't help wondering if there's some other source of your unhappiness. Like drink. Or pills. People often think drink is a symptom, they *like* to think it's a symptom, but sometimes it's the real problem and not a symptom at all. Or pills."

"I never take pills."

"It was just a thought."

"I do drink, of course, like everybody, but I'm not an alcoholic, if that's what you're implying."

"Of course not, but . . . "

"But what? But what?"

"Well, you do have that slightly bloated look that drinkers get sometimes."

Tears filled Dixie's eyes. "I can't believe you're saying these things. You've always been so kind."

"I'm sorry," Maggie said. "I truly am." And she felt sorry as she said it, but later she realized she was not sorry at all. These things had to be said. They were true. Dixie Kizer would just have to face reality.

Dixie Kizer had faced reality all her life and she didn't like what she saw. It was terrifying and she was not up to dealing with it and so she drank. What was so awful about that? Everybody she knew drank. It was a refuge, a place to hide, it was like her pink blankie when she was a baby. Her father had died young of cirrhosis and that's why she had all the money Maggie was so curious about. And her grandfather had died of cirrhosis too, now that she thought of it. It was sort of a family disease. Her mother hadn't died of it, at least not yet, though she probably would.

Her mother lived in Atlanta with her latest boyfriend. She had lived in New York and in Paris and in London with other boyfriends, and she still had apartments in London and New York, but this boyfriend liked Atlanta and so they lived there. He was Dixie's age and very handsome in a hired-stud sort of way and, since he was a painter, her mother had opened a gallery for him. They each had a schedule. He painted every morning and was very attentive to her the rest of the day. Her mother descended the stairs shortly after noon, bathed, refreshed, and flawlessly made-up, and the stud would be there waiting for her with a Bloody Mary in hand. Just to take the edge off. They didn't drink again until after five. The other boyfriends had provided similar services, and Dixie had accepted this life as reality. Boarding school and college she accepted as a kind of substitute reality. Her abortion and her breakdown didn't really count. They were unreal altogether. They never happened or at least they should never have happened.

So what was this nonsense about facing reality? She, after all, was the one who married Hal. *That* was reality. What did Maggie Tate know about it? She couldn't even pass her course in theory.

Still, Dixie reflected, she liked being with Maggie. Maggie was a kind of surrogate Philip. If that was as close as she could get, she'd take it.

She poured herself a stiff bourbon and stretched out on the chaise longue. Philip might yet change his mind and show up some night. She had not seen him in three whole weeks, but she believed in love. He might come to her, and soon. He might.

It was August and the heat was terrible. Ordinarily the Tates spent the month of August in London so that Maggie could see theatre, but this year she was taking her theory course and Philip had a couple essays he wanted to write, so they remained at home, working, sweltering.

Cole wrote from Hopkins and told them, telegraphically, his news. He was working on the immunology of white cells; very interesting, very important work. He had met a really great intern and they were sharing the cost of the apartment so he'd be saving money this summer and maybe in the autumn too, if they continued to share the apartment. He hoped they were both fine and that Mother's course was going well.

Philip read the letter and noticed that the intern's gender was not identified and decided, on the whole, it was better not to know.

Emma wrote from her island in Greece that the days were unbearably hot and the nights unbearably cold, but she was having the best experience of her life. It was very cultural. The other sand-sifters were okay and the work was exhausting. Bubby was the greatest. She hoped Mother's course was a big success and that she'd get an A plus at least.

Maggie read these letters and cried. The kids were great. The kids were loyal. But their expectations served only to make things worse. She had been working steadily on her paper for weeks and she was convinced it was a disaster. She told Philip this, and she told herself this over and over, and finally she decided to drop the course. "Don't do this," Philip said, "please don't," and he persuaded her to go and talk to Professor Ritson about the paper and simply ask her for some help. "But don't drop the course," he said. "It'll be the death of you."

And so, terrified and bucked up by a couple Xanax, Maggie went to talk with her professor.

"What's your point?" Phoebe Ritson said.

Maggie explained at some length the reading she had done in the early Faulkner, the thesis she had devised, the arguments she had used to develop her thesis, the texts that would substantiate it, the references, the footnotes, the intertextuality at issue here, but Phoebe Ritson interrupted and asked again, "What's your point?"

Maggie explained that she was trying to explain.

Phoebe Ritson listened for a while longer and then said, "Look. I'll read through your paper right now and give you some kind of preliminary report. I'll give you advice. I'll suggest revision. And that's a hell of a lot more than I'd do for anybody else, any normal student, I mean. I'll do it for you because you're older and you're a woman and you're coming back into the field and I want to give you a shot at it. I believe in sisterhood and all that. But you've got to do the work. You've got to summon the intellect and the spunk and the balls, so to speak. There's just so much I, or anybody, can do for you. You've got to save your own life, as it were. And if you can't, well then it's better to face it right now and get on with something else. Doing lit crit is not the end of the world, if you get me. Be an investment banker. Be a real estate agent. Be a cook, for God's sake. But if you're gonna do this stuff, lit crit, you've got to be tough. Okay?"

Maggie listened. Phoebe Ritson was a woman in her thirties and she was hot. She needed nobody. She controlled her own life. All hail, Phoebe! Maggie saw that she could never be Phoebe Ritson, that it was too late, that she simply didn't have the talent for lit crit. Nor for investment banking. Nor . . . but, as Phoebe would say, what's the point?

"Okay?" Phoebe Ritson said again.

"Got it," Maggie said, "A thousand thanks, Professor Ritson. You've made all the difference."

She went home and drank gin until she threw up. Then she took a Halcion and went to bed. Perhaps, with luck, she would never wake up.

It was almost a month now since Dixie had been alone with Philip and she decided she had to see him, to be with him. She had seen him at cookouts at the Fioris and the McGuinns. She had seen him at a performance of *Comedy of Errors* put on at

Brandeis. And she had seen him at his kitchen window one night at 2 A.M. when she drove by just to check on him. But she wanted to be alone with him. She wanted him on top of her, inside of her. She wanted to crush herself into him until she disappeared altogether.

She thought of Hal and his filth and his sick goings-on in Boston. He had told her things she didn't want to know and he had showed her the raw flesh of his groin and, just this week, the knife marks on his breasts and under his arms. Theda did it at last, he told Dixie. He'd persuaded her to cut him, just a little, and then she'd licked up the blood. Hal confided this slowly, patiently, holding her down on the bed, whispering that she could do the same to him, he would let her, he would help her, and he would only do to her as much as she wanted. He'd stop whenever she said to stop. He wouldn't hurt her, not really. He paused, his breath sour and hot. It would be the fuck of a lifetime, he said. But Dixie turned her face away, sobbing, and finally he let her go.

She hated hearing these things. She hated thinking about them.

The next night, though, as she lay on the chaise longue thinking of Philip, she imagined him bending over her, bearing down on her, hard, hurting. With a knife at her breasts? Licking the blood? It was revolting. It was the very opposite of the reason she loved Philip: he was so gentle with her. He was hesitant in making love, he held her softly, he kissed her with feeling that came from his heart and not from his groin. She lifted her glass and discovered it was empty. She filled it with straight bourbon—to heck with water—and took a long sip. Hal couldn't understand this kind of love. He had always been rough, grabbing and twisting and wrenching his gross satisfactions out of her body. He was a violent man, period. He liked to hit her. It was true that he had hit her only once, a fake hit intended to get her excited. But he was, he *was* a violent man. He was a potential wife-beater, a rapist, a killer. He was not beyond that. He *could* kill her. And it would be her right to defend herself. Women did that all the time these days. They shot their husbands, or set them on fire while they were sleeping, or just stabbed them to death. Maybe she *should* agree to his sex games. Tie him up with ropes around that disgusting thing of his, get his hands and feet tied to the bedposts, and then take a knife . . . It was all so clear and easy. She could do it. She could kill him. And she would get away with it too, they all did, the abused women who killed their husbands. She lay on the chaise longue, her eyes closed—was she sleeping or was she imagining this or, she laughed to herself, was she actually doing it?—and she saw him stretched out on their bed like the da Vinci model of man, and she saw herself draw the knife from his left nipple down to his crotch. And then from the other nipple down to his crotch. And then across his chest, a line connecting the nipples. She had made a perfect triangle on his body. She could press deeper and then lift the skin off his chest. She would do this. She straddled his body to make the work easier. She ran the knife over the lines she had made, pressing a little deeper, just a little more, and a little more. Fine. She loosened the flesh from his left nipple and then from his right, and she ran a finger along the line between them to loosen the flesh there, and then she began to peel it, slowly, down toward his crotch. It stuck a bit, but she worked slowly, tugging with both hands where that was necessary, and she found it was coming along nicely. She was fascinated by what she was doing and she was fascinated that it was such an easy operation. And necessary too. She should have done this a long time ago.

She sat back to examine her work. It was then that she truly saw what she had done. The huge triangle of skin was wet in her hands and she could smell the blood and she sat up, screaming.

Hal came down the stairs two at a time. "What?" he shouted. "What?" But he saw it was nothing, just the bourbon, and he sat on the chaise next to her and held her until the screaming stopped. He smoothed her hair. He kissed her on the neck. He pressed her head to his chest.

She put her arms around him finally and said, "Don't leave me, please. I'll stop drinking. I'll stop now. Don't ever leave me."

Maggie skipped the next two classes and when she returned it was just in time for the final exam. She had never seen anything like it. She had expected essay questions, of course, but these seemed not to be questions at all, but points in an argument she could not understand. "Structuralism divides the sign from the referent and poststructuralism divides the signifier from the signified. This is an obviosity. But it's implications for Derrida's *Limited Inc* as opposed, say, to Roland Barthes' *From Work in Text* require (de)lineation. N'est-ce pas?" She looked down the page and saw that the questions or essays or whatever they were got increasingly confusing. She had a headache from too many pills and too little sleep. She was sick to her stomach.

She took several deep breaths and began to write an essay on the word "delineation," breaking it down, stretching it out, free-associating with it. She planned to take it into other art forms—painting, sculpture, architecture, videotics—after which she would move backward into signs and referents, signifiers and signifieds, making informed guesses as to the content of *Limited Inc* and *From Work in Text*. A half hour later she sat back and looked at what she had written and saw it was gibberish. "Shit," she said, and did what she had wanted to do all along. She got up and left.

She wanted out, out of this exam, out of this world. She avoided the cafeteria where, she had no doubt, Dixie would be waiting and instead went straight to her car. She drove around Cambridge for a while and then took Mass. Ave. to Storrow Drive and out toward the airport. She began to cry a little, but she brushed away the tears and willed herself numb. She forced herself to think of the road and the cars and the fact that everything ends sometime, somehow, and this too would end.

She got to the airport but kept on going. She hit the stretch of the Revere Beach Parkway where they had porno movies and Lo-Ball bars, and she slowed down, looking for a place to get a drink. A lousy place. A dive. She pulled into Buck's Neon Palace and parked her car.

It was mid-afternoon and Buck's was nearly empty. Neon signs provided the only light and cast an unreal shimmer on the bar and the pool tables and the tiny stage at the back. Two rotten-looking kids were playing pool and an old Asian man was wiping down the tables. The bartender nodded to her as she stood in the doorway.

"M'aam?" he said.

Maggie squinted in the gloom for a moment and then she approached the bar and sat on one of the high stools.

"M'aam," the bartender said once again. He was tall and tough and he was looking at her as if she didn't belong here.

"Scotch," she said, "on the rocks."

"Johnny Walker? Chivas? Or the house scotch?"

She gave him her social smile, forgetting where she was. "House scotch will be fine," she said.

He placed the drink before her, on a napkin, and walked to the other end of the bar. He busied himself polishing glasses.

Maggie shifted uncomfortably on the stool. She had never been to a bar by herself, ever, and now that she thought of it, not with Philip either. They weren't bar people. Maybe that's what was wrong with them. Maybe that's what was "slowing things down" between them, as Philip had said. Slowing things down indeed. That fool. That idiot. He understood nothing. She looked over at the two kids playing pool and was surprised to see, now that her eyes had adjusted to the shimmering reds and yellows and greens, that they were not kids at all, just skinny guys in tee shirts and jeans with a lot of messy hair. They were in their twenties at least, maybe older. They had that druggy look. All bones, caved-in chests, pelvises at the ready. One of them was staring at her. She turned away and finished up her drink.

The bartender, without looking, seemed to know she was ready for another. He raised his eyebrows—a question—and she nodded. He poured her a second scotch and went back to polishing glasses.

She finished her second drink and waited for him to notice. He didn't. "Bartender," she said. He kept on polishing glasses. "Bartender," she said, more loudly this time. Still no response. She tapped the glass against the bar until he turned toward her.

"I need another drink," she said.

He came down the length of the bar and looked at her. "You all right?" he said softly. He looked straight into her eyes.

Maggie thought, I could love him, I could be somebody for him, I could make him happy. His face was squarish, pockmarked, and he had a thick sand-colored mustache. Forty or so. He was wearing a Hard Rock Cafe tee shirt and she wanted to put her hand on his chest, right where it said Rock.

"M'aam?" he said.

She returned his direct look. "I'm fine," she said. "Or at least I'm gonna be fine. It's been a very bad day."

As he poured her another drink, she said, "Buck's Neon Palace. Are you Buck?"

He passed the drink across the bar, thought for a moment, and then said, "Yes. I'm Buck." He stood before her, folded his arms across his chest, and then opened them and leaned back against the wall of bottles behind the bar. "Buck," he said.

Maggie felt her face flush. She shook her head.

He was looking at her.

It was her move.

"I'm sorry," she said. "I'm not myself." She put a ten-dollar bill on the bar. "Is that enough?" she said.

Buck nodded, looking at her still.

She left and drove home slowly, carefully. She took two Halcion and went straight to bed.

Philip stood by the bed and watched her sleep. She looked like death. He had seen this day coming—the final exam, her final failure—and he had done nothing to prevent it.

She was out, gone, and one day she would be gone for good.

Who was she? He didn't know any longer.

He leaned over to kiss her on the forehead. "Sleep," he said, and was horrified to hear in his own mind, just for a second, perhaps only a millisecond, "and never wake up."

13

Everything would be different from now on, Philip decided. He would make Maggie's emotional salvation the first order of business. Not teaching, not research, not writing, but Maggie first and only. He would become a different man, definitely. He would continue, of course, to be the loving, supportive husband who listened and cared. No, correct that, he would *begin* to be a loving, supportive husband who cared. He would listen, really listen, to her. He would anticipate her needs, her fears, her insecurities. He would make her feel loved and valued. He stood by her bed thinking these things.

And then he thought, What a crock of shit. He was a psychiatrist, for God's sake, and knew that emotional salvation is a personal thing, nobody can do it for you, you do it yourself or you're damned.

He went downstairs and made himself a gin and tonic. Rather a festive drink when your wife is laid out upstairs, unconscious, but it was late August and hot as hell and let them all go fuck themselves.

The problem, as he saw it, was that course in literary theory. It was gobbledygook, Maggie claimed, it was a way of making lit crit the private property of the indoctrinated, the blessed few, the tenured professoriate. Suppose she was right and theory was just gobbledygook. The fact would still remain that if she wanted to get her Ph.D., she would have to read and understand and probably even teach theory. And, as she was demonstrating at this very moment, she couldn't. She couldn't read it or understand it or teach it.

What she needed was a little more backbone.

How cruel he was and what a terrible shrink. What a terrible human being. "A little more backbone": there was not a manic-depressive, not a schizophrenic, not a serial killer in the world to whom he'd say such a thing. And yet here he was saying it to his own wife. Or at least thinking it.

He poured himself another drink and went upstairs and sat in her lady chair. He would keep vigil. And when she awoke, he would be loving and understanding. He would really try this time.

"I'm calling to ask how she did on the exam," Beecher said. "I know she did wonderfully, but I think it's nice to ask and give her a chance to talk about it, don't you? To dwell on it? It's not easy going back to school after all these years, believe me, I know, even though I never did it myself actually, but I mean I can understand it. Can I talk to Maggie and just ask her myself?"

Philip explained that Maggie was lying down. It had been an exhausting day. Perhaps she could call back tomorrow or the next day. Or sometime.

"Oh," Beecher said. "Oh, dear. That doesn't sound good at all, does it. Do you think it does? She didn't do well, is that it? And she's disappointed. Not *really* disappointed, I hope, not badly enough to give up on her degree. Oh, dear."

"Beecher," Philip said firmly.

"I should stop, that's what you're saying. I'll call tomorrow. I'll invite her to lunch. I'd like to be of some use, Philip, you know that. You *do* know that."

Philip said he knew that.

"Oh, dear," Beecher said and, reluctantly, hung up the phone.

Maggie woke that night and she did not know where she was. She kept her eyes closed and tried to remember. The last thing she could recall was some psychedelic bar, with a neon glow surrounding everything, and a feeling of terror that she would fall and keep on falling and never come back. And then, in a rush, the whole day returned to her: Buck's Neon Palace, the drive home, a lot of pills. And before that, the nightmare of the final exam. She covered her face with her hands and waited. Finally she opened her eyes.

It was dark in the room except for a small reading light over by the lady chair. She turned her head on the pillow and looked. Philip was sitting there, reading. She hated him.

"Hello, sweet," he said. "How are you doing?"

She closed her eyes.

"Can I get you something, Maggie? Some water?" He went into the bathroom and let the water run until it was cold. He brought her the glass and said, "Take a little sip."

She turned her face away from him.

"Not a little sip? I'll leave it on the nightstand and you can have it later if you're thirsty. Okay?"

He sat down on the side of the bed, carefully.

"Can I get you anything?" he said.

He said, "Are you okay?"

And he said, "Do you not want to talk about it?"

She said nothing and so he got up and went back to the chair and picked up his book. "I'll just sit here, okay?" he said.

She watched him for a while and then she got out of bed and went into the bathroom. She used the toilet and flushed it and began to open the medicine chest for a Tylenol. She stopped. He would hear her and think she was taking Halcion or something. She always kept a few drugs in the medicine chest to throw him off the trail; the big stash was in the closet hidden among her shoes. Still, he'd suspect something if he heard the medicine chest open and close. She went out and got into bed.

"Okay?" he said.

"So now you're spying on me?" she said.

"I'm concerned," he said. "That's all."

"And so you're spying on me."

"Maggie," he said.

"Maggie," she said, imitating the concern in his voice, exaggerating it, making it sound fake. "Maggie," she said again, and turned on her side and closed her eyes.

He sat there for a while, silent, and then he said, "I'll let you sleep. If you'd like some hot soup or something when you wake up, just call me and I'll make it for you. Okay?"

He went over to the bed. "Okay?"

She covered her eyes with her hand.

"You sleep," he said. He turned off the light and went downstairs to his study. He took down a paperback, *Memory in Chains*, and tried to read it, but it was sensational and at the same time predictable—case histories tarted up for shock value—and he sat there with the book in his lap, trying not to think.

Across the street and one house down, Dixie Kizer sat in her little MG, watching. She saw the light go off in the bedroom and then a moment later she saw the light go on in the study. They might be sitting there together, Philip and Maggie, reading, or perhaps even snuggling on the couch. Or the two of them in a big armchair, Maggie in his lap, Philip touching her breasts, gently, gently, the way he had touched her own on that night in the sunroom. But maybe Maggie was a drunk—she had been drunk that night at the Gaspards—and so Philip wouldn't want to touch her at all. No. He must be alone, studying or writing, trying to get back to his normal life, trying to forget they had had that one night together. But she could not forget. She would never forget. She resisted the temptation to get out of the car, cross the lawn, and lean in through the bushes and look. She would not do that to him. She would not let herself go that far.

She started the car and drove away, slowly.

Maggie did not come down for breakfast the next morning, so after a long wait, Philip brought up some coffee and put it on the nightstand beside the bed.

"I brought you some coffee," he whispered.

Maggie turned her face deeper into the pillow.

Downstairs he packed up his briefcase and was at the door ready to leave when he heard the shower upstairs. So she was awake. He would wait for her to come down. He would act perfectly natural. He would not mention a thing about the exam or about her being drunk or about anything at all. He'd just make her feel . . . good.

He checked his watch and then went to the telephone and called his office. He would be delayed, he told his secretary, and she would have to reschedule his first patient for another hour. He never rescheduled patients, so of course she thought it was some big emergency.

"Are you sick?" she said. "Are you going to be all right?"

He told her he was fine.

"Is there anything I can do? Anybody I can contact for you?"

He was fine, he'd be an hour late, that's all.

There was a little pause and she said, "Philip?"

She never called him Philip and something about the way she said his name startled him.

He laughed, a reassuring laugh, and said, "Hey, not to worry, I just have to reschedule an appointment. Be there shortly." And he hung up.

He was upset, though. He went into his study and sat down at his desk. He could see what was happening. He was becoming a different person and his secretary sensed it and was responding to it. He was in danger of becoming like one of his own patients, unable to see life because he could see only *his* life. Or rather *her* life, Maggie's. And that way they both would be lost.

Upstairs the shower stopped. So Maggie would be down in a few minutes and he should be busy at something and not look as if he'd been waiting for her. He shuffled the correspondence on his desk. Some bills, a catalog from Hammacher Schlemmer he'd been meaning to look through, postcards from Emma, a letter from Cole. He should write Cole and reassure him that everything at home was fine. He should write Emma.

But where was Maggie? There were no sounds of her moving around upstairs. Could she have gone back to bed? He moved from his desk to his chair and leafed through an old *New Yorker*. The cartoons were all familiar, and not funny either, and then he realized why. It was the same issue he had flipped through the night that he had driven around and around and ended up at Dixie Kizer's house. He got up and went to the kitchen and stuffed the magazine deep into the trash bag. Finis. Period.

He started upstairs and turned back. He went into his study and sat, deliberately turning the pages of the Hammacher Schlemmer catalog. The camping equipment. The maxi-humidifier. The electric nose-hair clipper. He read the description of each item and then checked his watch again. A half hour had passed.

He climbed the stairs, his heart beating fast, and went into the bedroom and stood by her bed. She was in a deep sleep, probably drugged. Her face looked troubled. He felt a twinge of annoyance, and then guilt, and then something that was probably pity though he hoped it was love. He left and went to work.

It was a long, anxious day.

When he got home, a little late, Maggie was cooking dinner—one of his favorites, scrambled hamburg and macaroni—and she looked rested and relaxed and beautiful.

"You look great," he said.

"Pour yourself a drink," she said. "This'll keep."

So everything was going to be fine after all.

They had dinner and talked about the kids. A letter had come from Emma, with rhapsodic descriptions of nightfall and sunrise on a barren Greek island and, mercifully, with no mention of Bubby. Cole had written about his research work, which he found occasionally boring but very fulfilling, and which had convinced him that research was his bag, not practice. "His bag," Philip said, rereading the letter, "his bag." Maggie smiled and said, "We've got to face it. English is a lost language." "Tell me about it," he said before he realized what he was saying. They changed the subject immediately.

And that was as close as they came to discussing her final exam in the theory course, or what happened afterward, or what would happen next.

Beecher Stubbs phoned early the next morning. She wanted to take Maggie to lunch and hear all about the final exam and the Ph.D. and everything else. Maggie said no. No lunch. Not yet. I'll call you, she said.

Dixie Kizer phoned in mid-morning when she was sure Philip would be at work and asked if Maggie would be at school this afternoon and could they have coffee at the student union? Classes are over, school is out, Maggie explained, so no, she wouldn't be going to the student union. Dixie dithered for a while and then asked if they could meet somewhere else? For coffee? Just to see one another? No, Maggie said. Sorry. An hour later, guilty, she phoned Dixie and made a date to meet at Starbucks at four.

And at noontime, Philip phoned and suggested they go out to dinner tonight, a treat, no special reason, just a dinner out, it might be nice. Maggie thought for a while and said, Yes, why not?

She was hanging up the phone when the doorbell rang and there stood Beecher Stubbs. She was wearing blue-green polyester pants and a billowing shirt, a lighter green, that reached halfway to her knees. She looked like a bag lady.

"It's me," she said, "a great big pixie," and she did a pirouette on the front steps. "A great big *old* pixie."

"Come in," Maggie said, but Beecher said no, she was on her way to a solitary lunch in Boston, a leaf of lettuce, some cottage cheese, an olive, something pathetic like that. She didn't want to intrude, she just wanted to see with her very own eyes that oh so lovely face and let her know she cared. That's why she stopped by. That was it. Period. So Maggie went to lunch with her after all.

"Well, it's perfect," Beecher said, "we've got the ladies who lunch, and I see a few of their daughters, very young, who must be in training, and there's a peculiar-looking man over near the buffet." Beecher made this comment, and similar ones, as they waited to be seated and then waited again to be served. Neiman Marcus, she pointed out, was still undiscovered by the tourists, at least the lunchroom was, and so it still provided the perfect place for a nice private chat. "And a very nice lunch too," she added as the waitress approached to take their order. Beecher ordered the *caneton a sauce l'orange* and Maggie ordered a Cobb salad. "These pants are stretchy," Beecher said, "a real find." She sat back then, looking at Maggie, and for once said nothing.

"You're an old friend, Beecher."

Beecher nodded.

"And you've seen us, Philip and me, go through a lot, I guess. Our first years here, they weren't easy by a long shot, and then Cole's paralysis when he was nine and Emma's anorexia and me not having a job and Philip's tenure in the middle of everything. You've seen it all."

Again Beecher nodded.

"And you've been a friend the whole time. You know everything about us, about me."

"And love you both," Beecher said.

"But this, now, I can't talk about this."

"No," Beecher said.

"I can't, I won't."

"No," Beecher said again. "No, of course not."

"You understand, I hope. I'm just trying to deal with it."

"Of course I understand and of course you mustn't talk about it." Beecher was not sure what Maggie was talking about, or wouldn't and couldn't talk about, but she was willing not to talk about it, whatever it was. It couldn't be the course in theory, that wouldn't make sense. It couldn't be Philip, could it? Well, could it? "Tell me all about Cole's research," Beecher said, "and about Emma's fantastic job on that Greek island, I think it's so exciting when your children get to do all the things you've wanted to do." She paused, wondering if she had just stumbled into it: your children doing all the things you've wanted to do. "Tell me about Cole first of all, because that's the least interesting. We can save Emma for dessert."

And so they got through lunch on the news about Cole and Emma, and the Med School budget cuts, and the new provost, and the possibility, the likelihood, of Philip becoming the new Dean. It was only after they parted that Beecher recalled she had not asked about Maggie's course in theory. Could that, conceivably, be what she didn't want to talk about? They would have to schedule another lunch.

Maggie changed into her beige slacks for coffee with Dixie. She started to ask herself why she was bothering, what it meant, and then said, Fuck it, and changed anyway. The slacks made her look younger. There was nothing to analyze about that.

Dixie was already seated at an outdoor table when Maggie arrived. Dixie was wearing white slacks and a blue and white shirt and she looked ready for a yachting trip. She had dark circles under her eyes.

"A latte," Maggie said to the waiter, "decaf, if you please." She sat down opposite Dixie. "And how are you?" she said.

"I've stopped drinking," Dixie said, "but never mind that, how did your exam go?"

"A breeze," Maggie said. "It went very well."

"Oh, I'm so glad. I'm so glad for you."

"Yes, well, I'm glad too. Tell me about this not-drinking business. You're not drinking at all?"

"No."

"Not anything?"

"Well, coffee," Dixie said, and lifted her cup.

"Why?"

"You told me I shouldn't. You said, 'You've got that slightly bloated look that drinkers sometimes get.' You said that."

"I shouldn't have. I'm sorry."

"So I stopped. Also it helps me with . . . other problems."

Maggie thought about that.

"And you asked me if I took pills. But I don't. I never have."

"Sorry."

"And you asked me why I don't leave my husband. And you told me to just *do* something."

"Good heavens. After all these terrible things I've said, I'm surprised you're willing to talk to me, let alone meet me for coffee."

"I know."

Maggie laughed. It was all so preposterous.

"But I like you. I like being with you." She looked at her coffee cup. "I wish I could be you."

Maggie shook her head.

"I do. You're so beautiful and smart and you've got it all together. And you're married to Philip."

"Yes."

"I wish I could be you. I wish I could *be* you."

"Listen, Dixie, I'm going to tell you something you should know. It may help you, though I'll probably hate myself for telling. Hell, I'll probably hate you for knowing. But here goes: I didn't do well in the theory exam. I didn't even finish taking it. I walked out."

"But you said . . . "

"I lied. It's too humiliating to talk about, but I want you to know this: I couldn't do it. I couldn't pass the course. I couldn't even understand what the hell they're all talking about. So when you're thinking you'd like to be me, keep that in mind."

"Why are you telling me this?"

"I'm giving you something. I'm being generous for once in my life."

"You didn't pass the exam?"

"I didn't even *finish* the exam."

"What did Philip say?"

"I didn't tell him. He doesn't know."

Dixie thought about this for a while, and then she said, "I'll never tell. I'll never tell anybody. Thank you for trusting me."

"I hope it will help when you're feeling down."

"I'm not drinking anymore."

"I know."

"And I've gone back to painting. I'm not very good, but I do it."

"Let's have another coffee. Shall we have another coffee?"

Maggie asked about the painting and she tried to sound enthusiastic, but already she had begun to feel sad. She had given away something—her weakness, her failure—and she could see that Dixie didn't understand what it was or how to use it. She would regret telling this woman anything. It was a mistake and she would have to pay for it. Suddenly Maggie felt hollow inside, in her stomach, in her chest. Even the coffee tasted bitter. She wanted out. She wanted a drink. At Buck's Neon Palace.

Nonetheless she asked more and more about Dixie's paintings and her art history study and when she might see the paintings. "Oh," Dixie said, "I would never show them. They're only realism." And that was the end of that.

Maggie looked at her watch. "I have to dash," she said. "Dinner with Philip."

"Lucky you," Dixie said.

It was five o'clock by the time Maggie got home. She had left herself time for a long soak in the tub, but she was upset about her talk with Dixie—she must have been insane to tell her about that exam, that nightmare—so first she poured herself a scotch and washed down a Xanax with it, and then she ran the hot water for her bath. She had finished her drink by the time the tub was filled, but the bathwater was much too hot, so she went downstairs and got herself another drink, a stiff one. She lay in her bath sipping the scotch, and when she was done, instead of dressing she decided to lie down for just a minute or two to rest her eyes. When she opened them, Philip was standing over her, looking anxious and trying not to.

"Taking a little nap?" he said.

"A teeny tiny nap," she said, and saw that he looked even more anxious. She wiped her mouth with the back of her hand.

"Good for you," he said. "A rest is good. Shall we get ready for dinner?"

"Have a shower," she said. "You'll feel better."

While Philip was in the shower, she went downstairs and had another stiff drink, quickly, in three gulps. She was at her dressing table putting on lipstick when he came out of the bathroom holding the empty scotch glass she had left there. He crossed the room and put it down in front of her. She looked at him in the mirror.

"So?"

"I thought you'd wait and we could have a drink in the restaurant."

"We can."

He frowned and bit back what he was about to say.

"Say it," she said.

"Sorry," he said. "I just worry."

"Well, don't worry about me. You've got plenty to worry about without worrying about me."

He looked at her in the mirror, searching out her gaze, but she was examining her makeup, avoiding him.

"Let's have a great meal," he said, enthusiastic, "and a great evening."

In the restaurant they ordered drinks and Philip attempted small talk about the day. The budget-cutting was finally beginning to affect the staff. Everybody was grumpy. Everybody felt ill-used.

"Everybody *is* ill-used," Maggie said. "It's the way of the world. Or at least the way of our cozy world here at the Medical Center," and she waved the waiter over for another drink. Philip had barely touched his and said he didn't want a second. "I'll drink alone," Maggie said. "I'm used to it."

The evening went on like this, a very long evening.

Maggie was drunk by the time they got home and Philip helped her upstairs to bed. He sat beside her, looking, until she opened her eyes and muttered, "Go away." Then he moved over to the chair by the window and sat in the dark, waiting.

After a while he went downstairs and poured himself a drink. He would have to do something for her, something definitive, but whatever it was, it would have to wait till tomorrow. He started into the study, but for no reason at all except that he wanted some cool air, he opened the front door and stepped out. He inhaled. Mown grass. Roses. He raised his glass and drank and as he did so he saw that across the street and one house down there was a dark MG with someone in it.

Quickly he went inside and closed the door. Then he went upstairs to bed.

14

"We've got to talk," Philip said.

"I know," Maggie said.

It was the next morning, a Saturday, and Philip had decided that desperate measures were required. Somehow he would have to get her to a psychiatrist. To McGuinn or to Fiori or, if necessary, even to that old fool Gaspard, but she had to see somebody, and right away.

"Will you see somebody, Maggie, just to talk about this?"

"Yes."

"Will you do it soon?"

"Yes."

"The kids will be here by the end of the week."

"I don't want to talk about it. To you. But I will see somebody."

"McGuinn is good, don't you think?"

She gave him a hard look.

"How about IHOP for breakfast?" he asked.

So Maggie went back to Leona Spitzer, her shrink.

"Where did we leave off?" Maggie asked.

"Begin anywhere," the shrink said. "You know where we left off."

Maggie was silent for a while. They had left off with the pills and the booze and the self-destructiveness. And with her anger at Emma and at Philip and at herself. And they had gotten no-where. And now she would have to tell her about flunking the course in theory.

"Take your time." Leona settled deeper into her chair. She was ready, if she must, to spend the hour in silence.

"I've met a man," Maggie said, astonished to hear herself saying this. "His name is Buck."

The hour went by very fast and when it was over, Maggie got in her car and drove past the airport to Revere and Buck's Neon Palace. She wanted to check the accuracy of her description.

The place was exactly as she remembered it: the neon haze shimmering over everything, a couple scraggly kids playing pool—four kids today—and Buck, solid and sexy behind the bar.

"Yes, m'aam," he said.

"A diet Coke, please." She blushed as she said it and rum-maged in her handbag so as not to catch his eye.

"One diet Coke," he said, and pushed the glass across the bar to her. "And will there be anything else?"

She shook her head. When she looked up, she was surprised and a little relieved to see he had walked to the other end of the bar. He was leaning there, watching the pool players. He had given no sign of recognition.

She drank her Coke quickly, put a dollar on the bar, and left. She was beginning her new life.

Maggie had not had a drink all week, and though she moped around the house during the day, she was pleasant and chatty when Philip got home each evening. He had still not asked her about her theory course, nor if she'd seen a shrink, nor how she was doing with the pills and booze. It was enough for him that something good had happened—she seemed happy, she seemed sober—and he didn't need to know exactly what it was, though he supposed it was her visit to the shrink.

On Thursday Philip was interviewed by the Dean's Search Committee and the interview went very well. Philip was a finalist, one of three, the only inside candidate. Did he want the job? How did he see his role in the new, tougher, tighter Med School? How did his family feel about it? His wife? His colleagues? And then later, alone, Aspergarter asked him in confidence if there was anything he should know about Philip's private life that could later become an embarrassment: any professional mishaps, for instance, any financial indiscretions, any personal problems? Sex? Drink? Certainly not drugs? He was sorry but he had to ask. A formality, but alas a necessary one, and totally, *totally* off the record. Philip assured him he had nothing to hide except . . . some time ago there was a . . . how to put it . . . a sexual indiscretion with a married woman. A one-time thing. It was past history, forgotten. Maggie knew and had forgiven him. Aspergarter pondered this. But it *is* over? Without repercussions? Absolutely. Absolutely. Aspergarter nodded and said yes, well, um, we all have one of those in our past, but just make sure it stays firmly in your past. A human weakness, probably not a bad thing. Finally he smiled. And how is the wife, how are the kids, young Cole and little Emma? Such great kids, so good-looking, so bright. The interview was over.

Emma and Cole arrived together on Friday. Almost at once they went out to look up friends. There was so much to catch up on. At night Maggie went into Emma's bedroom for a chat, but Emma told her she was too tired for a chat and, besides, what she did with Bubby was her own business. She did not want to talk about it, period. Cole got home long after everybody else was in bed.

On Saturday they all played tennis—a foursome, a family—and in the evening they went out to dinner. Maggie and Emma didn't drink, Philip and Cole had only a glass of wine with dinner. They talked about Cole's blood research and Emma's dirt-sifting and each of them was careful to keep away from dangerous topics: Maggie's theory course, Emma's lover, Cole's apartment mate. They talked about the possibility of Philip's being Dean of the Medical School. They talked about books and movies. They laughed. They were a happy, good-looking, well-adjusted family.

On Sunday, there was a garden party at the Kizers'—an end-of-summer celebration—and the whole department was invited. Philip said he wasn't going because his kids were home and he wanted to spend time with them, but Cole and Emma insisted he had to go because of his position as Goldman Chair and potential Dean of the Med School, and Maggie said she'd do what everybody wanted to do if they'd just make up their minds, and so they all went together. Besides, everybody agreed it would be fun to get a look at the Kizers' house.

It was a catered party with bartenders at a huge drinks table and waiters in uniform passing canapes. The whole psychiatry gang was there, even old Gaspard, and a bunch of physicians as well. Hal Kizer was playing the genial host, urging everybody to drink up and fight the heat, and Dixie moved from group to group, smiling and apologizing for the warm weather. She wore a pale yellow sundress and her black hair had just been cut Dutch-boy style and she looked young and fresh and very pretty. Maggie introduced her to Emma and Cole.

"I think you're so lucky," Dixie said to Emma, and to Cole she said, "Hello," and lowered her eyes.

Maggie couldn't help laughing at this new, flirtatious Dixie Kizer.

"Great haircut," Cole said. "Sort of the twenties." Dixie smiled, but did not look up at him. "It's really . . . great."

Maggie stopped laughing. It was one thing for Dixie to flirt with him but quite another for Cole to respond to it.

Beecher Stubbs appeared, talking. "My favorite people," she said to Dixie, and then she told Maggie how well she looked and Cole that he was looking very handsome and Emma, who in fact was looking fattish in a tee shirt that said "I dig it," that she wanted to hear every little last thing about her summer in Greece, it was too exciting, she simply had to know.

Cole suppressed a smile and Dixie saw him do it. They exchanged a knowing look.

"Let me get you a drink," Cole said.

"I don't drink," Dixie said. "I can't."

"Really?"

"I have a problem."

"Well, come sit and talk," Cole said, and they walked down the garden past the drinks table to a wrought-iron bench. The bench was uncomfortable, but it was private and it gave them a view of the entire garden. "This is very nice," Cole said. He saw his father look over at them from the drinks table and then, rather too quickly, turn away. Dixie saw him as well.

"Is this bad?" she said. "Should we join the others?"

"No, let's be bad."

They laughed, and Dixie said, "You're a lot like your father, I think. You're funny."

He smiled.

"And you're handsome. And kind."

"Tell me about this problem you have," Cole said. He was feeling handsome and funny and kind. "Go ahead. I'll play shrink."

The party went on around them, and people drank more than they should have and laughed too loud and ate a lot of things they didn't want. It was a big success and in a few hours it was over.

The drive home was very quick and nobody said much of anything: the party was nice, it was a bore, the food was marvelous.

As soon as they reached home, Cole got his father alone in his study.

"This is an outrage," Cole said, "and I demand an explanation."

"I was about to say the same thing."

"Dixie Kizer told me—"

"Dixie Kizer, exactly," Philip said. "Have you any idea how you looked today? Sitting alone with that woman for the entire afternoon? Quite apart from the rudeness to her guests, do you have any idea how it *looked*?"

"Please stick to the point," Cole said. "Dixie Kizer told me what's been going on here and I demand an explanation. I want to know why it is I have to learn from a perfect stranger that Mother flunked her theory course? That she never even finished the exam? That she walked out and she's probably feeling destroyed and suicidal, for Christ's sake, and you never even mentioned it to me? What are you doing about this? Are you doing anything about this?"

"Stop shouting."

"It's Mother's life I'm talking about and I'll shout if I want."

"I won't continue this."

They stood looking at one another.

"*Are* you doing anything about it?"

"I didn't know about it. She wouldn't talk about it."

"Jesus Christ."

"She's seeing a shrink. She's doing well, Cole. She just can't bring herself to talk about it. To me."

"To you she can't. To Dixie Kizer she can. Explain that, if you please."

"Well, I don't know what to say to that."

Emma opened the door and put her head in. "What's all the shouting?" she said. "Mother's gonna hear you."

"We're not shouting," Cole said, "we're discussing. Do you mind if we have a little privacy?"

"Well, excuuuuse me." Emma disappeared.

"That's supposed to be repartee," Cole said. "God, will she ever grow up?"

"She's grown up. Let me assure you, she's grown up."

They were silent a moment.

"Another thing," Cole said. "Do you have something going with Dixie Kizer?"

"Do you?"

"I'm not a married man. It's you I'm asking about. She sort of hinted at something."

"She's a troubled person."

"Is she your patient? Is that it?"

"Cole, for God's sake."

"Well, I'm not asking what she tells you on the couch. I'm just asking if she's a patient."

Philip shook his head.

"She told *me* plenty. Do you know about her husband? Hal? He's a perv. I mean, an S&M perv. We're talking heavy duty, chains and knives and shit. Don't you think you should be doing something to get her out of that deal?"

"What makes you think I'm in charge of doing something about the Kizers? They're nothing to me." He began to get red. "They're nothing to any of us."

"You are not facing up to your responsibilities, Father. These women need help! Mother needs help, goddam it!"

"Time out. Time out. You aren't talking, Cole, you're just venting. Why don't you go upstairs, take a shower, then come down and we'll very calmly, very logically, discuss this. Okay?"

There was a knock on the door. "Tap, tap," Maggie said, leaning into the room. "You fellas okay?"

"How are you, Mother? Are you all right?"

Maggie looked at Philip and then back to Cole. "What do you mean?"

"I mean just that. Are you all right?"

"Yes, I'm all right. Why should I not be all right?"

Emma came in. "You see. I told you she'd hear all the shouting. Why does everybody in this house always have to shout?"

"What's going on?" Maggie said.

"There's nothing going on," Philip said. "We were trying to have a discussion and we raised our voices and now Cole is going up to shower and we're going to talk about it later. Okay? Okay."

"Is this about Dixie Kizer? You spent the whole afternoon with her, Cole, it was really a disgrace."

"Cole thinks he likes older women," Emma said. "Big deal."

"As a matter of fact, not that matters of fact interest anybody around here, what Dixie Kizer and I were talking about was you, Mother. And what Father and I—"

Emma interrupted. "Faaather," she said. "He calls his father Faaather."

"What Father and I were talking about is why he's not doing anything to help you, because quite frankly I think . . . well, I think he's not being supportive enough."

"Your father and I handle our own problems, thank you."

"Oh yeah. Oh sure," Emma said.

"Well, you handle them in a rather peculiar way, it seems to me. You don't tell Father you've flunked your theory course, but you tell a complete stranger like Dixie Kizer. How do you explain that?"

Maggie felt her face go red. She looked at Cole and then at Philip and then back to Cole. She shook her head. Tears rushed to her eyes.

Everyone was silent.

"Well," Maggie said, and she tried to say something else but the words would not come. She laughed, a small broken sound. She left the room slowly, as if she were sleepwalking.

They all remained silent as they listened to her passing through the kitchen, going up the stairs.

"I hope you're satisfied," Philip said.

"I happen to value the truth," Cole said. "It's something I might recommend to you."

"God, what a house!" Emma said. "I'm so fed up with living in a dysfunctional family. Why don't you all just kill one another and be done with it. Now *I've* got to go up and see if something can be done about Mother. It's always me, me, me!"

Emma went out and slammed the door.

"God!" Cole said. "Deliver me from shrinks!" And he went out and slammed the door as well.

Philip went to the door, opened it, and closed it again softly. He sat down at his desk to try and think.

It was after midnight. The phone had rung once and somebody picked it up before it rang a second time and then there was silence. Now, as Philip watched from his study window, he saw Cole leave by the front door and go down the walk. He crossed the street and went left and disappeared from view. A moment later Philip saw a dark MG pass in front of the house, slowly.

It couldn't be. Cole would not be that crazy. Even Dixie would not be that crazy. But there was no limit to the irrational, Philip knew.

He took one of Maggie's sleeping pills, but it was a long time before he fell asleep.

15

Dixie lay on the chaise longue in the sunroom, happy and, for once, satisfied. She had wanted to talk with Cole—simply talk with him, nothing else—because he was so sympathetic and young and untouched. And he was a wonderful talker. He listened. And he seemed to care. This is how Philip must have been in med school before he got so thoroughly professional, with his ultimatums: I can't see you, this must never happen again, if you threaten suicide, I won't come, I'll call the police. Philip was inhuman compared to Cole.

She had intended only to talk with him, but she was very happy at the way things had turned out. She was in love.

She wasn't deceiving herself. She knew this had to be a one-night affair. It was never meant to be an affair at all. At the garden party that afternoon she had told Cole all about . . . well, everything. She told him about Hal and his sex seminars, she told him how terribly alone she felt, she told him how wonderful it was to talk with him. Hal, she said, would be off to the city again tonight, he always went after a party like this. And she would give anything just to continue this talk. Cole said he would be glad to talk. And they did.

She had phoned him shortly after midnight and a few moments later picked him up in her car. It was so easy.

Cole was a caring person. He said it was a crime for Hal to treat her this way. Hal was sick, he said. He said she should get out of this marriage. Simply get out. And then, after quite a long while, he had touched her hair, and massaged her neck a little, and eventually he had traced her mouth with the tip of his finger. After that she had to touch him back, his face first. It was nearly Philip's face, but very young and clean and almost beautiful. They kissed and she was ready to move on to anything he wanted, anything at all, when suddenly he startled her by saying, "Shall we have intercourse?" "Intercourse?" she said. "Should we fuck, I mean, or do you want to just, you know, mess around?" "Intercourse, please," she said, and Cole continued on, slow and passionate, as if there had been no interruption at all.

Cole. Cole and Dixie. If only she had met him ten years earlier. But of course that was silly because he would have been in sixth or seventh grade. And she would have been in the loony bin. Think of it.

When she was fourteen and ugly, she discovered that she could step out of the time that everybody else was in and just be very peaceful. They thought she was there with them, but she wasn't, she was watching them from a distance, apart, above them. After a while, when she had been gone long enough, she could come back, and then she would be in the same time as the rest of them. But while she was out of time, she was safe. She did this often, secretly, at boarding school. When she went away to college, she did it less often, because for some reason she was less scared. But when she got pregnant by her psychiatrist and when, at his insistence, she had an abortion, something strange and nearly final happened to her. She stepped out of time and decided not to come back. It was the most peaceful period of her life.

She gave up eating and drinking, she gave up walking and sleeping, she gave up speech. She sat by her window in a rocking chair—where, she wondered now, did the chair come from? —and she rocked and she closed her eyes and she opened them. She had stepped out of time for good. Her roommate nagged her and then pleaded with her and finally got the resident fellow to take a look, but nobody could do anything with her. Her psychiatrist came and talked to her privately but he couldn't seem to get through. He warned her that he could have her committed. Another doctor came. And another. You're in pain, they told her, but they were wrong. She was not in pain, she was in the absence of pain, she felt nothing. Nothing at all. After a few days they put her in a mental hospital, and fed her, and made her drink. They made her do finger-painting. They made her sit in a group of other crazies and say what it was that frightened her. Loneliness, she said, because that was what they wanted to hear and because she had decided she wanted to get out. I want to belong, she said, and they were pleased. I want to be like other people. I do. I want to be like other people. She said it so often they finally let her go. Home to Mother and Mother's stud of the moment, the Paris one, or maybe the London one.

The next year she went back to college and studied art history—time, with a vengeance—and got a job as docent in the Gardner Museum. That was where she met Hal, whom she married, and thus became a doctor's wife who played piano and went to museums and gave catered garden parties. Then she'd met Philip Tate. And now Cole.

Cole was another version of Philip. Younger and taller and—she couldn't help thinking it—he was a better lover. He was bigger down there for one thing, or at least he used it better. Men thought women didn't care about size, and mostly they didn't, so long as the man knew how to use whatever he had. But that was gross and she was not being fair to herself. It wasn't sex she was interested in, it was love. And she'd done it—she'd gotten him, she'd made love, real love, with him— without resorting to alcohol or seduction or anything. She'd taken Maggie's advice and she'd *done* something and she'd done it sober.

Perhaps she could do anything she wanted. Leave Hal. Get a career. But what career? Well, she could begin by leaving Hal. Or at least not thinking about Hal. She concentrated, deliberately, on Cole's long body stretched across hers, his heavy thing dragging against her flesh, moving slowly, a wonderful light and animal weight. He was only twenty-two or twenty-three. He was what she needed. She could become a normal woman with him.

Maybe Hal would die and she would not have to leave him. Maybe one of these nights in the city he would go too far, cut too deep. Sometimes they did it in the bathtub, he and Theda, in the water. She didn't know you could do it underwater, that it was even possible. Maybe he would drown. By accident, of course, but dead anyhow, and out of her life. She thought of that awful dream where she had peeled his skin away, off his chest, from nipple to nipple and down to his crotch. She closed her eyes against the picture of it. All that blood. She tried to erase the blood but keep him dead.

Hal pulled off the freeway and lay his head on the wheel and for a short while drifted in and out of sleep. He and Theda had gone too far or not far enough, depending on how you looked at it, but it was terrific. Fabulous. The only problem was that he'd not given himself enough time to recover before getting into his car to drive home. He'd be more careful next time.

Theda had promised him this wild British thing; apparently all the Brits were doing it. Actually, about ten years ago, some Member of Parliament had snuffed himself doing it, but that was because he did it alone and he did it wrong. With her watching over him, he could get the orgasm of a lifetime and not have any risk at all.

She made him lie down on the floor—it had to be a flat, hard surface, she said—and she attached this wire to him. It was just picture frame wire, but it was coated with some plastic thing so it wouldn't cut, and she wound it around his big toe first of all, and then around his dick and his balls, once around each, and then brought it up to his neck. But the big thing was that she put a plastic bag, very loose, over his head but *under* the wire, so that all he had to do was bear down on his toe, flex his foot like he was stepping on the gas, and automatically he'd tighten the wire around his whatsis and also around his neck, cutting off just enough oxygen so that the brain would do a loop-dee-loop and his dick would go absolutely wild. And you had complete control over it. All you had to do was bring your toe back to normal, as if you were taking your foot off the gas, and you got some oxygen and you caught your breath and you made sure you were okay. Once you were ready for more, you only had to put the old foot on the gas and you were all set to roar again. It was the infinite orgasm. And here was the best part. You took a little wedge of orange and you squirted a tiny bit of amyl nitrate on it and you put it in your mouth and left it there. You couldn't help biting down on it as that wire tightened. And then, ecstasy.

Don't worry, Theda said, it's all under control. She'd watch over him. She'd make sure the plastic never got too tight around his face. She'd see to it that he didn't come to death, ha ha ha.

Theda was right. It was the best he'd ever had, an orgasm that started up and up, and then paused right near the top while you got your breath again, and then started up from there, going higher and higher, until near the end Theda herself couldn't stand just watching it and she unhooked the equipment and climbed on top of him and finished him off.

It was great, it was the greatest, but it had messed up his breathing. No heart problem. No lung problem. He wasn't worried about that. He just had trouble keeping awake. So he pulled off onto a side street and dozed. After a while he slept, and then he woke up and drove home, within the speed limit, very careful and precise.

* * *

Dixie had given up picturing Hal dead. She was remembering Cole, sweet Cole, and their one-night stand. But this could not be the end. She wouldn't let it be the end. She would take Maggie's advice and do something.

The back door rattled and the kitchen lights went on. Hal was home. She could hear him at the refrigerator pouring something into a glass and then she heard a cabinet bang shut. The kitchen lights went out and he was suddenly by her side.

"Well?" she said, disgust in her voice.

Hal was silent, but when he spoke his voice was raspy and he seemed out of breath.

"You should be in bed," he said.

"I haven't had a drop to drink," she said.

"Come on, mousie." He gave her his hand and helped her up from the chaise longue. "Come on." And with his arm around her, they went upstairs to bed.

16

"Can we have a talk? I think we should have a talk?"

"Let's do it. Let's talk."

They had just finished watching the six o'clock news and, since they would only be having cereal for dinner, there was no need to worry about the meal getting cold.

"I'm sorry. I know you hate these things, Calvin, but I feel you have to talk with me, you have to be open. All right?"

"Good God."

"Do you think we have a good marriage, Calvin? Not comparatively, but for real."

"Yes I do. Don't you?"

"You don't have yearnings?"

"Beech. Everybody has yearnings."

"Well, I mean yearnings for something different. Or better."

"No."

"Well, for some*one* different or better."

"Sweetheart, what's the matter, what's happened?"

Beecher's eyes filled with tears, she blew her nose, she swallowed hard. "It's just that . . . I'm fat . . . and you're still attractive, and I wonder . . . "

"Come here," he said.

"No. No, I don't want any of that now. It's too easy and it's too . . . well . . . easy. And I have to get to the bottom of *me*."

"What do you want to know? What do you want me to say?"

"About the fat, first of all."

"Oh God," he said, miserable. "You're overweight, Beecher, that's true. But it doesn't bother me, I sort of like it, and it's never bothered you until now, so I don't think your weight is the issue here. Do you?"

"See, you're so smart, Calvin, you're so insightful. That's why I love you, that's one of the reasons. But you've aged so well, men do that, and women just get older and saggier and, well, not very interesting. And it affects the marriage."

"I think we have a very good marriage," Calvin said. "We're not the perfect marriage—who is?—but we love each other and we respect each other and we enjoy being together. At sixty-eight, that's pretty good."

"I'm only sixty-seven."

"At sixty-seven and sixty-eight, that's pretty good."

They didn't speak for a while.

"Oat Squares?" Calvin said. "Is it time?"

They continued to sit in silence and then Beecher blurted out, "You don't think I'm just comic relief?"

He got up from the couch then and knelt down by her chair and put his arms around her. He kissed her on the lips.

"I think you're comic, in the sense of funny. I think you're witty. I think you're utterly without malice or meanness or spite."

He paused to see how she was responding, but her eyes were closed and she seemed to be concentrating hard. He went on.

"And you're a relief to come home to every night. You're a relief from the pettiness and meanness and selfishness and . . . and the ambition and arrogance and . . ." He put his hand on her cheek. "What brings all this on, anyhow?"

"Oh," she said, "I'm a preposterous old woman, gadding about and having lunch and talking too much and invading people's privacy and it occurred to me at the Kizers' garden party that when people seem to like me, it's only because I'm comic relief."

"Give us a kiss," he said.

"Calvin, don't be absurd. We're old people. And this is serious."

"Everybody is comic relief to somebody," he said. "They all star in their own lives, everybody does, and the rest of us provide comic relief."

"But nobody ever sees me the way you see me. Nobody ever sees that I might be serious, that I might have a real life."

"Who ever sees anybody else, completely? We never *know* anybody."

"Oh, Calvin, that's awful."

"It's comic."

"I suppose."

"We just happen to be lucky that we found each other." He got up off his knees, awkwardly, and then he helped Beecher up, and they went into the kitchen to prepare their dinner—tonight it was Cracklin' Oat Bran.

They ate in silence for a while.

"Oat Squares," Calvin said, "What more could anyone want?"

"It's true," Beecher said. "This is the life."

17

They had not spoken in a day and a half. The kids had left, with feeble attempts on all sides to pretend that everything was okay, but now Philip and Maggie were on their own. Philip was determined they would talk.

"So much for the news," Philip said, as Dan Rather said good night. He clicked off the television.

"Don't you want to watch the local news?" Maggie said.

"It's just the same news, only twice as long."

Maggie shrugged and said, "I'll get the dinner."

"Sit here," he said, "would you, Maggie? Please?"

"I'll get the dinner. We have to eat, no matter what, I suppose." But she continued to sit there on the couch. She was very pale.

"I'm sorry. I'm sorry about what Cole said to you. I'm sorry he hurt you. I'm sorry *I* hurt you."

"You don't know . . . ," and her face crumbled. "I felt like . . . I felt like some kind of animal that's been run over in the street . . . I . . . You don't know, you could never know." She began to sob. She buried her face in the sofa pillows, her body shaking, and her sobs grew louder. He put his hand on her back, soothing her, but she shook more violently and the sobs became more awful, more terrifying.

Philip had cared for the criminally insane and for manic-depressives at the apex of mania and depression, and he had looked deep into his own dark mind, but he had never seen anybody so abandoned.

"You don't know," she screamed.

Her desperation shook him. It would break her. He couldn't endure it.

"No! No!" he said, and there was panic in his voice, a desperation like her own. He clutched at her, he wrenched her body from the sofa into his arms and crushed her to his chest. "No," he said, softer now, and held her close, soothing her, waiting until the hysteria passed.

The hysteria did pass finally, and they sat together on the couch, unable to talk, unable even to feel. After a long while Maggie slept, cradled in his arms, and Philip held her, determined to stay there forever if necessary, determined, in his way, to save her.

The next day was unreal, of course, and they both acted as if last night had happened weeks ago. They ate breakfast mostly in silence.

"So you'll be all right today? While I'm at work."

Maggie said she would be fine.

"What will you do? Will you see your . . . person? Your shrink person?"

"Tomorrow. But I'll get through today. I'll prepare my grade book and go through my notes, you know."

"Sure, sure."

"I'll get ready for my first class."

"Sure. And I'll come home at noon, okay?"

"No!" she said, too loud, and assured him again that she would be fine.

"Is it okay if I phone?"

"Do what you want," she said. "You will anyway."

He got his things together and prepared to leave for work.

"I'm sorry," she said. "I know you're trying to help."

Once he was gone, Maggie felt emptied out. She hated him being there, looking at her, pitying her, but she missed . . . what? Did she miss anything about him, or was he just a habit? Old Philip, good-looking and smart and caring—God knows, he was caring—but there was something about him she hated, or at least resented. His pity. Philip and the others, Cole and Emma, all of them pitying her.

But she must not let herself think this way. She must not let herself think at all. She got up quickly and rinsed the breakfast things and put them in the dishwasher. She bathed and dressed, mechanically. She went downstairs with her books and papers as if she were going into a classroom.

She made neat piles on the dining room table: her grade books for the past seven years, old syllabuses, photocopied handouts: on the sentence, the paragraph, the thesis, the development of the thesis. She looked at the accumulation of papers and said aloud, meaning to be funny, "Maggie Tate, this is your life!" But it wasn't funny. It was, like her life, pitiful.

She went into the kitchen and took an aspirin and drank a glass of water. Just buck up, she told herself, it can be done.

Back at the dining table, she took her yellow legal pad and sketched out class readings and home assignments for the first week. The big thing was to challenge them and engage them. To show them that good writing was simply good thinking, clearly and forcefully expressed. Elegance could come later. Clarity was where you had to begin. What exactly do you mean? Well, say it.

"Say it," she said, and sat back and looked around the room. It was a nice room, with an old mahogany dining set that had belonged to Philip's mother. There was a hutch with their good wedding china, a liquor cabinet where they stored gift-wrapping stuff, and lots of extra chairs. They could seat twelve. Perhaps she should give a dinner party.

She picked up the pile of grade books, weighed them in her hands, and put them down. She flipped open the top one, from last year. The grades made a perfect curve, though she didn't believe in curves. It had just happened that way. Two As, six Bs, six Cs, two Ds. John Pottle and Juli Corrida got Ds. Did they care? Did they go home and get drunk or take pills or think about suicide? She tried to make herself feel something for them. Fat John Pottle, eager to please, a toady in the making. Juli Corrida, who only wanted to get laid, and did, without doubt, ever day of the year. Did she feel anything for them?

She went out to the kitchen again and this time she filled the water glass with vodka. She took a sip and leaned against the sink. The vodka burned the back of her throat. She hated the taste of it. She stared out the window at nothing and took another sip.

"God, what a mess," she said, and emptied the glass into the sink. She returned to the dining room to make one last attempt. She would draw up a syllabus, clear and effective, she could at least do that. She worked for an hour, made a cup of tea, then worked for another hour. She read over what she had written. It was good. It was done. She read over her flyer on grading, to be distributed on the first day along with the syllabus. "An 'A' paper (1) must have a point to make, a thesis, etc. etc. (2) must engage the interest of a reasonably intelligent and informed reader because it has some importance in itself and because the writer has given it a rich development with, for example, cogent logic, illuminating analogies, etc. etc. (3) must have a clear structure suitable to the etc. etc. (4) The syntax must be sound, the style lively. A 'B' paper lacks one or two of these etc. etc." Preposterous. This, from the woman who had just flunked a course on theory, the woman who had never read Husserl.

Again she went to the kitchen, and this time she measured a single shot of vodka into the glass, added orange juice, and drank it straight down. Then she went to the phone and called the college. There was family illness, she explained to the department secretary, she would need to miss class—often—all during the fall. Could they get a replacement? Just for this quarter? They would try. They thought it likely. Oh good. Oh thank you. Oh thank you very much.

She put away her notes and her offprints and her grade books. She would not be needing them again soon, maybe never. She went upstairs and took a Xanax and put on makeup. Just a little to give herself some color. Then she went down, poured herself a real drink, and picked up the phone.

"Philip?" she said, "I just called to say hi." She was twisting the phone cord around her hand, a little drunk, and she smiled into the mirror above the phone. "Well?"

"Hi," he said, and there was the crackle of fear in his voice. "Are you okay? I mean, is everything okay?"

She was silent, angry.

"Maggie? Are you there?"

"Yes, I'm here."

"Oh, well that's good. How is everything? I mean, you sound . . ."

She gave him time to go on, but there was only silence on the line, and finally she said, "You can't do this to me. You can't do this."

"What? Do what?"

"You can't always be suspecting me—you're suspicious, you're always spying on me. You think I've been drinking, don't you! Don't you?"

"No."

"Well, that's what you're implying. 'How are you. Are you okay? Are you all right?' Why don't you come right out and say it: 'Have you been drinking?' God!"

"I'm sorry. I didn't mean that. I just meant . . . I didn't mean."

"Well, don't do this to me."

"No, I won't. I'm sorry."

"I'm going to go now. I'm having lunch with Beecher."

"Oh good, that's good."

"So if you call, don't expect me here. I'm out with Beecher."

"Right."

"Good-bye, Philip."

She hung up the phone and continued to look into the mirror. Liar. Cheat. She shook her head. Poor Philip Tate, Goldman Professor of Psychiatry. Poor Maggie Tate, Nothing. Poor everyone.

Maggie went to the Co-op and bought groceries. Fruit and vegetables, some hamburg, chicken breasts, steak. Granola. Spaghetti. Peanut butter. Bread. Was she forgetting anything? She bought stone ground wheat crackers and some Stilton cheese. Milk. Ice cream. She took it home and put it away, in the cupboards, in the fridge, the dutiful wife and mother.

She went to the cleaners and picked up Philip's shirts. She bought black shoe polish. She bought extra batteries for the alarm clock. She hung up his shirts and she left the shoe polish and the batteries on the kitchen counter.

And she left a note that said, "I'm leaving you. I'll come back when I can, if I can."

She went to the liquor store and bought a half-gallon of vodka. She checked into the Ramada Inn. She went to sleep.

* * *

It was late afternoon, about four, when Maggie entered Buck's Neon Palace and sat at the bar.

Buck nodded to her.

"A scotch," she said, "a house scotch, on the rocks."

He looked at her just a second longer than he needed to and she returned his look. He got the drink for her.

After her second drink he just stood there with his arms crossed.

"What do you think?" he said.

Her mind raced. Was this an offer? Was she thinking of taking it? Was she losing her mind?

"About?"

"Anything," he said. "What's your sign?"

"I don't usually do this," she said. "This sort of thing."

"What sort of thing?"

She smiled.

"Slumming, you mean?"

"Drinking. In a bar."

"You usually do it at home?"

"Touché."

"Another?"

"I've still got some. I'm pacing myself." She looked around the bar, at the pool tables that were empty now and at the little stage near the back. "Who comes here?" she asked.

"People. Drivers, migrants, some Vietnam wrecks in the afternoon, drinkers. It's a different crowd at night. Some locals just come in for a drink, I've got a couple regulars, rich drunks from Beacon Hill who hide out here, folks from Brookline come out sometimes to see how a little lowlife would suit them. You know the kind, they're not sure the Neon Palace routine is camp or sincere. Lots of people come here. Just people." He leaned away from her. "Where are you from?"

She didn't answer.

"More to the point, what are *you* doing here?"

"Having a drink?" she said.

"I might be tempted to think you're looking for a little action, except you aren't the kind of woman who comes in here looking for action."

"I'm ready for another drink now."

He poured it and stood there looking at her.

"What do you mean by action?"

"An-y-thing-you-want." He sang it.

She took a sip of her drink, but when she put it down, her hand shook and some scotch spilled on her fingers and on the bar.

"Here, allow me," he said, and he took her hand and raised it to the light. He made a tsking sound and folded three fingers into her palm and touched the tip of her index finger with his tongue, quickly, perhaps a joke. She did not take her hand away. He pulled it closer and did it again, looking at her and she looking back, and for a moment everything was quiet, uncertain.

Anything could happen and she would let it. She wanted it to happen.

Then the door opened and two men came in.

She pulled her hand away and looked down at the bar. She tried to speak but her voice would not come. Finally she said, "I'm sorry. I really am," and she got down from the stool and left. She had forgotten to pay.

It was late in the afternoon and Philip knew he couldn't call home so he decided to phone Calvin Stubbs just to see how he was doing. Calvin was an old friend and they did not get together often enough and he just thought he'd check in with him. Besides, he might be able to find out if Maggie was okay.

Beecher answered the phone.

"Philip," she said, "what a delight to hear your voice. I was just saying to Calvin that we never see you anymore, you and Maggie, and we should have a dinner party. The problem is I'm not sure if I remember how to cook anything and I can't very well serve guests Cracklin' Oat Bran. But never mind that, how are you, Philip? And how's Maggie?"

Philip paused, but only for an instant. "I thought you had lunch with Maggie? No? I must have got the day wrong."

"No. Oh no. But we can take care of that right now. Put her on the phone, and we'll make a date straightaway."

"Well, she's out right now. I thought she might be with you actually."

"Oh. Well, no."

"It's not important, Beecher. I just needed to ask her about . . . Well, it's nothing, really, please give my best to Calvin, okay?"

"You bet, Philip, lots of love, bye bye." She hung up the phone and turned to Calvin and said, "Oh Calvin, things are *so* bad for the Tates."

Philip, meanwhile, sat looking straight ahead. He couldn't call home. He couldn't go home. He couldn't call around and try to find out where she was. In fact, maybe she *was* home, still working on her classes for the fall, or maybe she was out photocopying, or maybe she was just taking a nice nap, no drugs and no drinks involved.

But he knew it wasn't so.

Things had come to a place where there was no going back. He was married to somebody with a major drinking problem. No, let's say it: he was married to a drunk and she was doing nothing to save herself and only she *could* save herself. So what use was he, what good was he? He could threaten and cajole and bribe. He could leave her and at least save himself. Get out. Get out of this trap. Be, if there was such a thing, free.

Tears came to his eyes and after a while they began to trickle down his face. He wiped them away. The fact was that he loved her. Her and only her. And all the other lunacy—the drives in the night, the brief and guilt-ridden sex with Dixie Kizer, the rage at Maggie and Cole and Emma—all of it was only a symptom of his hopeless love for this maddening, tortured, self-destructive woman. He wanted to kill her and kill himself. He wanted to lie down with her and die.

And then it came to him that there was only one thing he could do. He must find her and love her, as she was, as she was determined to be, just love her. Dying didn't belong in the equation at all. And if you didn't know how to love, you could pretend, and if you pretended long enough—who knows?—it might turn into love. "Lie down in the rag-and-boneyard of the heart." What was that from?

He stopped crying and he sat there, hoping for something, anything, hoping the phone would ring.

At the Ramada Inn Maggie took a long bath and then she poured herself a vodka and Sprite and turned on the television. It was six o'clock, with news on all the major channels, so she flipped through the cable shows until she found an old Joan Crawford movie, black and white, with lots of suffering. After a while she turned off the sound and just watched the pictures. It was very funny, really, but she didn't feel like laughing.

Philip would have found the note by now.

Maggie got up and took a Halcion and lay on the bed with her eyes closed. Eventually, she figured, she would either sleep or die, it didn't matter which.

* * *

Philip was about to leave his office when the phone rang. He picked it up at once, without waiting for his secretary to say who was calling. It must be Maggie, it had to be. But it was not.

It was Aspergarter, calling on behalf of the President and the Provost and the Search Committee to tell Philip that he was their unanimous choice for Dean of the Medical School. He paused and waited for Philip's reaction.

"Oh," Philip said.

"I presume," Aspergarter said, "that means you are speechless with pleasure."

"Yes, of course," Philip said.

"And that you accept, with gratitude."

"Yes," Philip said.

"Well," Aspergarter said, "you certainly do manage to keep your emotions under control."

When Philip said nothing, Aspergarter went on to say that Philip's official appointment as Dean would not take place until the first day of the new year, so he should not expect any public announcement—the newspapers, the television— until January first, but of course he should feel free to tell his friends and relations and his fine, fine family. Then Aspergarter offered his personal congratulations, and assured Philip of his admiration and esteem, and, clearly disappointed, he hung up.

Philip went home to tell Maggie the good news that he had been chosen as Dean of the Medical School. No news had ever seemed so trivial.

He stood on the front steps and looked around. Wide lawns, old trees, a solid, established neighborhood. No murders here, no molested children, no scandals of any kind. He took a deep breath and went inside. He found Maggie's note on the kitchen counter. "I'm leaving you. I'll come back when

I can, if I can." He knew what it must say even before he read
it. Nonetheless he read it several times. And then he sat down
to think.

Maggie slept, and when she woke she took another drink, and
then she slept some more. Eventually, one way or another, it
would end.

Philip was determined to remain calm. "Please let her be
all right, all right, all right." He muttered this over and over
as he sat, trying to think, and after a while he realized he was
praying. Anything, he said to himself, so long as she's all
right.

There was no point in phoning the police. He could
scarcely say she was a missing person, since that was her ex-
plicit intention, nor could he say he was worried about her
because she might be drunk or on pills or just plain suicidal.
Nor could he think of anybody else to call. Beecher? Dixie?
The kids? Not on your life.

He got in the car and drove down to Harvard Square. Maybe
he would see her walking or see her car. He drove to Somerville
and then to Medford and then out to the shopping mall. Seven
o'clock, so of course nobody was around. Just people going home.
He drove over past the Stubbses', but there was no sign of her
car, and he couldn't find the courage to knock and say, Help
me, I've lost Maggie, she's left me. He drove by the McGuinns,
the Fioris, the Aspergarters. He was driving home when he
thought of the Kizers. Surely she wouldn't go to Dixie at such
a moment. But who knew? Who knows? He drove to Winchester and cruised by Woodlawn. Hal's Mercedes was in the
long driveway, but there was no sign of Maggie or her car. He
drove home.

There was a message on the phone machine. He punched the play button and waited, hoping, but it was only Beecher Stubbs with a message for Maggie. I haven't seen you in ages, we must have lunch, and on and on. He was angry and frightened and he wanted to cry, but he had no tears and besides he had to keep his wits about him, he had to think what to do next.

He thought of calling Cole. Cole was the one she would tell, if she were to tell anybody: I'm leaving him, Cole. He screwed Dixie Kizer and he's a self-satisfied shit and I'm through with him. And Cole would say, It's been my experience, Mother, that trouble of this kind starts in bed. Are you and Father having trouble in bed?

It was nine o'clock now. He phoned Cole and got the room-mate, the intern. A male. "Cole isn't here," the roommate said. "I don't know where he is, but it's still early so I presume he's at the lab."

It would be six o'clock at Berkeley, and Emma would probably be at dinner, but he called her anyhow just to ask how she was doing.

"I'm studying, what do you *think* I'm doing. Is something the matter? Is this about Mother? Or are you just checking up on me?"

Maggie was fine, he said. He just wanted to say hello to his own daughter and hear how she's doing and was that so strange?

"Let me talk to Mother."

"She's out," he said. "She and Beecher Stubbs went to a lecture. I'll have her call you tomorrow."

"Oh."

"Well, you take care," he said.

There was a pause and then she said, "If you're checking up on me, Dad, if that's what this is all about, you might want to know I've broken up with Bubby."

"Well, that's good. I'm glad to hear it."

"He's a dork. All men are dorks."

"Well, you take care," he said again.

"God," she said, "when will you realize I'm a grown-up?"

Philip paced the living room for a while. He went to his study and shuffled the papers on his desk. He went upstairs to the bedroom and looked through her closet. All her clothes seemed to be there, though the stash of drugs she kept under her shoes was missing. The liquor was still in the cereal cabinet but that didn't mean anything since you could get booze anywhere. She was off on a bender, that must be it. "Please let her be all right," he said aloud, and he was aware that this time he was praying.

He thought of phoning up motels and asking for her. Is a Mrs. Tate registered there? Would they tell him? Would they put him through? And then what would he say?

He got in the car again—it was nearly ten o'clock now—and he drove to Harvard Square and doubled-parked while he ran into the Motel 6. At the reception desk he said, "Excuse me. I'm supposed to meet a woman who's registered here, I *think* she's here, and I'm not sure whether she's registered under her married name, which is Tate, or if she uses her business name, which is Cole. C-o-l-e, Cole. Could you check that for me?"

He was saying too much, he sounded fake.

The kid at the desk didn't seem to recognize fakery, or didn't care, since he turned away from the miniature TV he was watching and, without a glance at Philip, punched up the computer and, sighing, said, "Cole, Cole, Cole," and ran his finger down the screen. "Nope." And then he checked Tate. "Nope," he said, "sorry 'bout that," and turned back to his television set. "This is so great," he said, smiling at the television, as Philip left and went out to his car.

He checked every hotel and motel around Harvard Square and then he moved on to Memorial Drive and he even tried one motel in Boston. Defeated, he returned home. There were no messages on the answering machine.

He showered and went to bed and lay there awake.

He was sleeping soundly, though, when the phone rang. The room was full of sunlight and the phone kept ringing and for a second he realized something terrible had happened but he couldn't remember what it was. Then it all came back to him.

"Yes," he said, snatching up the phone.

It was Beecher Stubbs and she sounded very unlike herself.

"Philip," she said, and her voice was slow, tentative. "I'm calling about Maggie. I got a call from Maggie and frankly, Philip, I don't know what to do. And Calvin doesn't know what to do. We decided we should call you."

"Yes," he said.

"She's not well, Philip. She's very bad, poorly, I think."

"Yes."

"She's at the Ramada Inn. In Revere."

"Thank you, Beecher," he said, about to hang up.

"Wait, Philip. Wait. It's like this. She said she was ill, Philip. She said she had left you and you didn't know where she was and I wasn't to tell you, but that she was drunk—it's the word she used, Philip, and I'm sorry to say that she sounded as if she might be—and that she needed help. And this is the problem, I don't know whether I'm betraying her, her confidence I mean, by telling you this or whether you should know and you should do something about it, and Calvin doesn't know either."

"Thank you, Beecher. I can never thank you enough."

"She's in Room 124, Philip. And Philip? She's registered under the name of Dixie Kizer."

Philip was silent.

"We love you both, Philip," Beecher said. "I hope she won't feel I've betrayed her."

* * *

Philip went straight to Room 124 and knocked on the door. There was no answer. A cleaning woman came out of Room 133 pushing her cart of linens and Philip called to her, "I've come out without my key. Could you open my door for me?" He indicated the room with one hand and with the other he reached for his wallet. He gave her a big smile. The woman shook her head, frowning, but she opened the door for him and took the ten-dollar bill he held out. "Have a nice day," he said. She gave him a look.

Inside, he locked the door and put on the chain. The room was dark and smelled sour. The television was on, with the sound off, but there was no one in the bed watching it and there was no one in sight anywhere. He went around the bed to the bathroom. She had vomited on the tile floor and he turned away from it quickly and shut the door. That was when he saw her, lying between the bed and the wall, her nightgown hitched up above her thighs, her face contorted. He knelt beside her. She was breathing roughly. He took her pulse. He felt her neck, her cheek, her forehead. She would be all right. She was lucky she had thrown up.

He pushed hard against the bed and moved it farther away from the wall. He lay down beside her. He touched her hair.

"Maggie," he said, very softly.

He took her hands in his and held them against his chest.

He lay his forehead against hers.

He closed his eyes.

After a long while he felt her hands move in his, and he felt her pull away from him.

"It's okay," he said. He was whispering.

She opened her eyes and looked at him. There was a moment of panic as she tried to see where she was, what she was doing here, and then her eyes clouded and she gave a little smile.

"Poor Philip," she said.

"It's all right. Everything's gonna be all right."

"You poor bastard."

"I love you. I love you," he said. He put his arms around her and drew her close. He said nothing else.

After a while she said, "I'm a drunk."

"It's all right," he said.

"I tried to kill myself."

"You're here," he said. "You're alive. You'll be all right."

She lay in his arms, silent.

"Maggie?" he said. "Take me back?"

She moved away a bit but she said nothing.

"Will you?"

"I don't know."

"Please?" he asked. "Take me back?"

FOUR

18

The big news that autumn was old Gaspard's daughter. Suddenly, just before the case went to trial, Helena "Tippi" Gaspard dropped the molestation suit against her father. At first Ms. Gaspard—she insisted reporters call her Tippi—would say nothing about her reasons for dropping the suit, but after a short while she gave a telephone interview to the local paper admitting that her father had never molested her in the technical sense. The technical sense? Reporters wanted to know what that meant. They requested another interview. They requested an interview with old Gaspard. They requested an interview with her psychiatrist. Tippi refused, and Gaspard refused, and the psychiatrist was said to be out of town at a conference. A couple weeks went by with no further requests from reporters. Tippi called a press conference to announce that she was suing her psychiatrist, a Dr. Lila Koren. The local television station requested a live interview. Tippi agreed and spent a lot of time preparing: she got herself a new hairstyling and a Mizrahi suit and she practiced her story in front of the mirror. She was a new Tippi. For the first time in her life she was lively and talkative, with disturbing anecdotes about Dr. Koren's psychiatric techniques, her deliberate distortion of facts, her conviction that all fathers were by nature child molesters. Did Dr. Koren actually say that? Well, practically. That was her message. That was her mission. That was her plan to take over the world. Dr. Lila Koren had no comment; the whole thing was too absurd, she said. Sally Jessy Raphael called and invited Tippi to appear on a television special called "Women Raped by Psychiatry," but Tippi said she would have to think about that. There were the legal aspects of the case to be considered and besides she had heard on the sly that Somebody Very Big in talk shows might be calling her, in which case . . . well, she said, she would have to take a rain check. Everybody was talking.

Everybody was talking about the Gaspards, and only a few people were talking about the Tates. And thank God for that, Aspergarter said, because he, for one, did not want to go through the rigmarole of searching for and appointing a new Dean. He had earned his retirement and he wanted out of the job. He wanted to relax and read books. And Philip would make an excellent Dean. Excellent. He genuinely liked Philip. Philip was, he said, a strange, highly principled, nearly brilliant young psychiatrist who had genuine gifts for administration. And of course, Aspergarter said, he wished Maggie the best. He was very fond of Maggie and she was being very brave about her problem.

Maggie's problem, though anything but secret, was very little talked about. Her many friends were protective and, despite her tart tongue, she seemed to have no enemies at all.

There were whispers, of course, that something awful had happened, a debauch at some motel or a fling with some raunchy bartender or something sexy and exciting that really wasn't believable, but nobody had any facts except that Maggie may have been at McLean Rehab to dry out and she may have moved into an apartment in downtown Boston during late September. Just for a while, a week or two, and then she went back home to

Philip and they patched it up. There was no doubt about the fact that she was in A.A.

In fact, much of the speculation was true. Maggie had signed herself into McLean for a minimum of two weeks but left after eight days, distraught, and determined this would never happen again. She found the place a prison, with lots of meetings to make you feel good about yourself, and vitamin shots and healthy food and smiling, smiling, smiling attendants. She couldn't bear it. She wanted her own bathroom and some privacy and something or someone . . . she didn't know what. Because of the way she had signed in, she had to petition Philip to sign her out. She did, and he did, and at her request he found her a furnished apartment and he helped move her in. "Don't call," she said. And so she entered her new life.

"My name is Maggie and I'm an alcoholic," she said as she paced around the new apartment, and by the time she got to her first meeting, she had accepted that fact as something she would live with and control. Accepting it—"I'm an alcoholic"— did not make the days, and especially not the nights, any easier. She woke up each night with horrible dreams. She was drunk on the motel-room floor, she was drunk and naked and dancing on the stage at Buck's Neon Palace, she was drunk and lashing out at the smiling attendants of McLean or at Philip or at Dixie Kizer. But she went to her daily meetings and forced herself to say her name was Maggie and she was an alcoholic, and by the end of the week she was ready not only to face the truth but to tell it.

It was her fifth meeting. "My name is Maggie and I'm an alcoholic," she said. Her voice sounded very loud in the room. People shuffled. Somebody coughed a lot. Some man said, "Welcome home, Maggie." She cleared her throat. "This is my first time talking about it, about the problem, about"—she had to force herself to say it—"about my drinking problem." Having said that much, she was able to say a great deal more. She muddled through her story and said it was a nightmare to be here and then she sat down. Somebody applauded and the chairman thanked her and she looked around, startled, because she saw for the first time not just a bunch of drunks but a group of people who seemed to be genuinely on her side. She smiled and they smiled back. Still, she could never really be one of them.

Two weeks later she returned home to Philip.

"Will you take me back?" she said.

"It's the other way around," he said.

She let herself be kissed and then she drove back to the apartment and picked up her clothes. Philip was at work and she ran a hot tub and soaked in it, with no pills and no booze and—could this be true?—no desire for any.

She might, after all, be truly home.

Philip negotiated these weeks like a sleepwalker. He went for advice to Calvin Stubbs, to his old buddies McGuinn and Fiori and, once he found out that she was Maggie's psychiatrist, he went to Leona Spitzer. They all told him the same thing. It was Maggie's problem. You may be part of the problem, you may be the excuse she uses from time to time, but the problem is hers, Philip, it's hers, not yours, it's hers, hers. He had never felt so useless in his life.

He did, however, what they urged him to do. Nothing much. Keep out of her way. Let her make all her decisions. Don't provoke her, don't spy on her, don't cover for her. And, Leona told him, get yourself off to Al-Anon. He did.

What struck him first about Al-Anon people was how many of them seemed to hate the person who had driven them there. "My alcoholic," one man said, referring to his wife, contempt in his voice. And a woman responded, "*My* alcoholics—

I've got two of them, both my mother and my father—*my* alcoholics are exactly the same. They lie. They're the best liars
in the world. They can hide liquor anywhere. Sometimes I
want to kill them. Frankly, sometimes I just wish they'd drink
themselves to death." Philip got up and left. But he came back.
Gradually he began to see that for a long time now he had
felt the same way. She was in a trap, yes, but her trap had created a nightmare for him. He too was trapped. And he hated
her.

He didn't hate her, he only wished she wouldn't do this to
herself, he only wished he hadn't driven her to it. Had he? No.
Yes.

He hated her and he hated himself and for a moment he was
tempted to say "Why me? Why us?" But he knew the answer
was "Why not?" and that was called fate or life or God's will,
but whatever it was, you had to live with it.

He didn't hate her and he didn't hate himself. He just had
forgotten how to hope. He would have to learn to hope.

Maggie had left McLean, and she had left the apartment in
Boston, and she was home again: wasn't this cause for hope? He
was afraid to hope. But he hoped nonetheless.

At Al-Anon they warned him to expect a relapse. There was
often a relapse. A 75 percent chance of a relapse. Count on it.
Thanks a lot, he said.

But he continued hoping and he continued going to meetings and if this wasn't hope, it was as near as he was going
to get.

One morning at breakfast, though he had intended never
to do this, he made the first move. He reached across the table
and took Maggie's hand in his and said, "I love you. I do."

And she said, "Thank you, Philip," which wasn't quite as
much as he expected. But by now he had learned to expect little,
to be grateful for anything.

* * *

She was beginning, finally, to feel she could survive these meetings. "My name is Maggie; I'm an alcoholic." This did not cover the ground, it did not tell the world who she was, but she wasn't here to deal with the world. She was here to deal with her problem and then, and only then, with the world. Calvin Stubbs assured her this was so and he was an expert.

She gave her little talk—my personal rap sheet, she called it—and she listened to the others give their little talks and she came to see that after one or two drinks they were all the same. Lost, she said. Done for, she said. Awash, Calvin said.

Her rap-sheet talk became more relaxed; she let her feelings out, she showed her anger. They nodded and said, Good, Maggie, very good. But Calvin said, I'm not so sure about those feelings.

"We alcoholics have short memories," Calvin said. "We've put our drinking behind us, and we get to feel that if our families don't do the same, they're not playing fair with us, they're not being good sports. They forgive us and we resent it. We forget that we're the ones who need forgiveness."

"I'm the one who's been through it," Maggie said. "He's been out . . ."

"Out?"

"Screwing Dixie, if you want to know. I'll never forgive him." And then she added, whether it was true or not, "Never."

"But he's forgiven you."

"Men," she said. "You're all the same."

"I love you very much," Calvin said. "But you're cold, Maggie, and you're proud of your coldness."

She bit her tongue and said nothing.

"I'm afraid for you."

"Isn't it something about Gaspard's daughter," Philip said.

They were lying in bed reading companionably.

"On TV all the time," Philip said.

"Well, she's getting attention, and that's what they all seem to want," Maggie said.

"Poor Gaspard," he said.

"Poor Bartleby," she said.

He smiled, because he knew it was a literary reference of some kind and he hoped, he hoped.

19

"Love and sex," Philip said aloud, "love versus sex." He was thinking of Hal Kizer, whom he was about to interview in preparation for taking over as Dean in January. He had never really talked to Hal. They had business exchanges, of course, and they served on committees together when they had to, and they had shared a couple chats—ugly, both times—when they were guests at department parties, but Hal was somebody Philip chose to avoid whenever possible. Hal was obsessed with sex, kinky sex, and he seemed to want Philip along for the ride. Philip didn't care to think of what this might mean. In truth, he didn't care to think of Hal Kizer at all, since everything about Hal made him uncomfortable.

Maybe he wanted to keep him a caricature: the kinky shrink with his balls in a Cuisinart, someone easy to dismiss. Maybe if he got to know him, maybe even to like him, maybe even to find his sex research a legitimate subject of inquiry, then he might have to take him seriously. And what would that mean? The enemy should never come alive as people: the first rule of combat.

His secretary buzzed him on the intercom. "Dr. Kizer is here," she said, and in a second Hal was standing before Philip's desk, smiling, his hand out.

Philip came around the desk, welcomed him, and they sat facing one another in the matching leather armchairs. This was to be a democratic encounter.

"We've never really talked," Philip said.

"So let's."

"I'm trying to get the feel of the job," Philip said, "so I've asked everybody on staff to stop in and say hello and tell me what their chief concerns are for the school and for themselves and, frankly, to express any reservations about me as Dean, if they have some."

"I don't have any. I think you'll be great." He reached down and adjusted his crotch. It was a spontaneous gesture. It meant nothing.

"Good. Well, that's good."

"How is Maggie doing? Dixie hasn't mentioned her lately, but I know they used to see each other quite a bit."

"Maggie's doing fine. Thanks. She's fine."

"Dixie's given up drinking," Hal said.

"Well, in the history of civilization, drinking hasn't done much good for many people, taken as a whole."

"I like a drink, myself."

"Yes, well, you do wonderful work, Hal. We're very lucky to have you here." He wasn't up to this but he launched into it anyhow. "Why don't you give me a sense of your research, Hal, where you think it's going, where you hope it might go. Just a rough outline."

Hal didn't pause to think. He just began. "Officially, like yourself, I'm an expert in manic depression," he said. "I'm interested in cognitive therapy, of course, but I'm more interested in what mood elevators can do with depression—I don't mean right now, necessarily, but with the next generation of pharmaceuticals—and I'm interested in the nature of the highs. Not so much in controlling the highs—bringing them down, smoothing them out—but in taking a good long look at them. What they allow to be created. What enlargement of spirit they make possible. What they imply about the inner life, about the soul."

"Very interesting."

"It is interesting, I think."

"The soul, you say."

"Of course I'm not Catholic, like you."

"Jewish?"

"Nothing. Not lapsed from anything. Not aspiring to anything." He paused for just a moment and then held Philip with his look. "Except sexual highs."

Philip blushed. He was over forty and men over forty didn't blush, it was a scientific fact, but he blushed nonetheless.

"Sexual ecstasy, to be exact. Or maybe just ecstasy through sex."

"Yes, well, you've indicated that before."

"And?"

"And, frankly, it's just not one of my interests."

"You could give it a try."

Philip shook his head.

"You could try it with me." He put his hands up, a surrender. "Relax, relax, I don't mean *with* me. I mean you could come along with me on one of my little seminars, just give it a whirl. The girls are very careful. They know what they're doing and they stop as soon as you say stop and—"

"I'm sure."

"What you've got to understand is this, Phil: I'm not hooked on sex as an end in itself. What matters to me is where it takes me. You Catholics like to rise above the flesh and find some kind of ecstasy in denial of feeling. I'm working the opposite way. I'm trying to go through the flesh, *through* it, to an ecstasy that's totally human and fulfilling. A mortal ecstasy. I don't believe in denial."

"I see."

"And I suspect you don't either."

"I'd like to change the subject, Hal, okay? S & M isn't something I like to talk about, or hear about for that matter, and it certainly isn't something I intend ever to try."

"Like Dixie."

Silence. Philip looked surprised.

"Dixie doesn't like it either. Or she thinks she doesn't."

More silence.

"You and I are not that different, you know. Our problems, I mean, and our solutions to them. We're both at that moment in our lives when things can go anywhere. I want my life to expand. I want . . . more."

Philip stood then and walked back behind his desk. He flipped open his appointment book, looked at his watch, sat down at the desk.

"I'm trying to be honest with you," Hal said. "I'm trying to show you who I am as a man, as a person."

"Of course. I know that. Of course. But I'm more concerned right now about the professional aspects, the purely medical aspects, of the research we're engaged in. Tell me about the developments you foresee with pharmaceuticals and the depressive cycle. That interests me a lot."

And so they filled out the hour with talk about manic depression and the future miraculous stuff that would make Prozac and Thorazine and Stelazine look like Alka-Seltzer. But at the end of the interview, as Hal rose to leave, he said, "About the other stuff, Philip . . . ," and at once Philip interrupted him.

"Yes, yes, I'm glad you mentioned that. You want to make sure that the other stuff, as you call it, doesn't get in the way professionally. You see what I mean. I mean, the Med School doesn't need another scandal . . . with Tippi Gaspard and molestation and all. The world at large is not ready for S & M."

Hal smiled and decided to give up trying to explain. "Gotcha," he said. "There'll be no scandal here."

Philip saw him to the door.

Hal Kizer *was* a caricature. Talking about the spirit, the soul, the inner life. My God, the man's entire inner life existed twelve inches south of his belt. He was a disgust.

That enemy will never come alive, Philip thought, not if I can help it. Hal didn't deserve to be taken seriously. He was a totally dispensable human being.

Without thinking what he was doing, Philip went to the bathroom and washed his hands.

Dixie was stalking him, but she never approached him. Philip was grateful for that. He worried only that she would approach Maggie. As it happened his worries were misplaced. It was Maggie who approached Dixie.

They met for coffee at the student union.

"We should have gone to lunch," Dixie said. "That's what Beecher and I do and we like it a lot."

"Beecher is very nice."

"You've stopped drinking, she told me."

"Beecher didn't tell you that. She wouldn't, not behind my back. I should imagine a lot of people know I've stopped drinking. Any one of them could have told you."

"Somebody told me, I thought it was Beecher."

"It wasn't."

"You look awfully good."

"I look older. I look a little beat up, but I've made it this far and I'll make it the rest of the way."

Dixie looked at her. "Cole is so proud of you," she said.

Maggie started to say something, stopped, and said something else. "The reason I asked to see you is part of my recovery. I have to apologize to everyone I've hurt through my drinking. And I've hurt you."

"Oh no."

"Well, I intended to."

Dixie's eyes filled with tears.

"And I apologize. I was working out my own insecurities

on you, attacking you on drinking and so forth, and what I really wanted to do was kill you. And you know why."

"Philip, you mean."

"Well, I'm sorry. And I apologize."

Dixie was thinking about killing. Maggie wanted to kill her and she wanted to kill Hal. Maybe Hal wanted to kill Philip. Maybe Philip wanted to kill Maggie.

"Do you accept my apology?"

"Of course, of course."

There seemed to be something still unsaid. Maggie bit her lip and looked around the cafeteria and then back at Dixie: she was beautiful, but hopelessly dependent and insecure. She was pitiful.

"You can do anything, you know. You *should* paint. You are a very artful woman."

"I'm beginning to see that," Dixie said. "I'm beginning to believe it."

Maggie stood up. "Well, thank you."

"Can we have lunch sometime? Soon?"

"Dixie," Maggie said. "I've apologized. I've said that you're artful and able. That's as far as I can go. My amends do not include lunch."

"You're an inspiration," Dixie said. She went home and phoned Cole and told him how well his mother was doing.

That night, as she often did, Dixie got into her MG and tooled around town for a while. She stopped at an art supply shop and looked in the window. She drove to Harvard and walked through the Square. And then she drove home.

After Hal had gone to bed, she went out again in her car and drove to Philip Tate's house. She parked the car down the street a little. She walked back and crossed the lawn and peered into his study window. He was not there. He must be upstairs with Maggie. She waited for a while and then she returned to her car.

As she was getting in, a heavy Mercedes pulled up behind her, slowed, and then sped up. She could have sworn it was Hal. But that was impossible, because Hal was at home in bed. Nor was he smart enough to think of following her.

When she got home, Hal's car was in the garage just as it had been when she left. She went inside to the sunroom and lay on the chaise longue. She put her fist firmly up between her legs and, gouging it deep into her, thought of Philip and of Cole and of Philip. She fell asleep finally and dreamed of Cole.

Upstairs, Hal lay in bed thinking. Dixie had more life to her than he had guessed: driving around town in the middle of night, peeking into Philip Tate's windows. Maybe even fucking him? No. Not uptight Philip. He'd run if she made the offer. He'd fight her off if she put a hand on him. And yet she was a queer one, all right. This pleased him greatly.

He had married her because of a misunderstanding—he had given her more credit for subtlety and sexual awareness than she deserved—and it had been many unhappy months before he realized his mistake.

She was a docent at the National Museum at a time when the treasures of the Prado came on a tour of the United States. He was fascinated by the late Goya, his grotesques and his bloody-mindedness, and he was amused by the cool, disinterested way Dixie, on her guided tour, introduced the paintings. She was sexy and detached and she seemed to take the gore and the madness as historical peculiarities, with no odd or disturbing element about them. They did nothing to her, whereas they made Hal's flesh tighten on his bones. He found himself physically excited by them. And therefore by her. He wanted to mess up that hair, yank up that dress, and take her right on the floor beneath *Maja Nude*.

He went back a second and a third time. He made chat with her. He said suggestive, harmless things. He moved closer. She remained cool and indifferent. He found out she had studied painting, was a painter herself, and he guessed she had money, lots of it. Sex and money and a taste for Goya. He returned for a fourth visit. After the tour, he waited for her and was surprised to see that she was waiting for him as well. "I've got something to show you," she said. "This picture is you. Pure you." And she led him to the early Goyas and paused before *The Manikin*. On the tour she had explained that it was one of numerous designs for a tapestry, more in the mode of the rococo in its gaiety, with almost no trace of the violence and madness Goya was to paint later. It was a joyful painting, witty, with interesting psychological overtones. Now, alone with him, she said, "Isn't it you? Really?" But he barely looked at the painting; he already knew it. It was sadomasochism masked as gaiety. Four women were tossing a man in a blanket. They were laughing, having a good old sexy time for themselves, and the little man, their victim, was sailing high in the air, his arms stiff, terror on his face. *He* knew what was going on—he was a sexual plaything, a penis dandled on the blade of a knife. Hal couldn't stand it. He touched himself and he was hard, and with his hand there he looked straight at her and said, "It's me?" She said, "It's you."

For the first time Hal felt he really knew himself. This was what he wanted, this dandling on the knife blade. And she knew it. And she liked it. She was not deceived by him. He thought, This one knows me, with this one I can explore it all.

Much later—indeed, too late—he discovered she had found the picture merely playful, a man having a good time with four women, somebody who was, she said, "a party kind of guy." By then, of course, it was too late. They were married and she was frigid and he began to look for his dandling outside the house.

Still, tonight, she had suddenly turned interesting. Following Phil Tate, peeking in his windows—she *must* be after his body, there was no other explanation. For some reason this excited him. He got up and went downstairs and found her on the chaise longue as usual, her fist between her legs, a look of satisfying pain on her face. Why couldn't she let him do that for her? Why couldn't she just give it a try?

"Come on, mousie," he said. "Beddy-byes." And he woke her from her very pleasant dream.

Maggie had trouble sleeping these days. She would go to bed exhausted, and then wake after an hour or so, full of nervous energy, edgy and excitable. Sometimes she lay there waiting to fall asleep again, but lately she had been getting up to read. Tonight, as Philip got into bed beside her, she was sleeping soundly, but within minutes she was awake and restless. She started to get up.

"Don't," he said. "Stay here and read. I'll just close my eyes and doze."

"But the light," she said.

"It's nice with you here," he said, smiling, his eyes closed. "Never mind the light."

She read for a while and then, seeing he was still awake, laid her book across her chest and said, "I wonder why she ever married him."

"Hmm?"

"I wonder why they ever married."

"Dixie, you mean? And Hal?"

It was the first time in a long time they'd had the same thought without expressing it. They were both pleased.

"Mm," she said.

He opened his eyes and looked at the ceiling. "I had an interview with him today. He's a brilliant psychiatrist. I know that from looking over his appointment papers and therefore I have to believe it, but my God, what a mess he is as a person."

"She's the one that puzzles me."

"I know."

"You don't mind talking about her?"

"Well, if you want. Do you think it's a good idea?"

"I don't mean the sex thing. I mean what she *is*. She's a rich woman, she's beautiful, she's had all this art education and she's been a docent in a major museum. And now she's painting. In oils. How does she come by this defenselessness thing? Is it a pose?"

"It's her attraction."

"You mean men like this poor-little-me routine? I thought that went out in the thirties. Or at least in the fifties."

"I imagine Hal liked it."

"Did *you* like it? Is that what made you . . . you know . . . have the affair with her? The fling?"

Philip saw the opportunity to confess. He could tell her now and have it over with, finally, for good. It would be an easy thing. He could say the words, just the simple honest words: as a kid I broke into houses. I don't know why. It was irrational and thrilling and I did it. I did it again at Dixie Kizer's house the night of the Aspergarters' party. It wasn't sex, it was . . . unreason.

If he told her, if she knew, if he knew she knew, it might never happen again. It couldn't—he'd be in her power.

"Should I not have mentioned it?" Maggie said.

"I was thinking," he said. "I confess I just don't know."

They lay there silent for a long while.

"I just don't know," he said again.

He rolled away from her and closed his eyes, waiting for her to turn off the light.

She waited too, to see if he would say "I love you" as he did all the time now. She thought of what Calvin Stubbs had said to her about short memories and forgiveness and about being cold. But she was not cold. She wanted to forgive him. She wanted to love him. If only he would say something, anything, something.

Minutes passed and neither of them said anything and she turned out the light.

20

Maggie was silent at breakfast the next day and Philip was silent too. He was thinking that he should have told her about the housebreaking, he had missed the perfect opportunity, he was a shit. She was thinking that she should not have mentioned his fling with Dixie Kizer, she should not be jealous of it, it meant nothing. She had forgiven him. She had to get on with her life, one day at a time, even though she was depressed and didn't feel like getting on with anything at all. So they ate in silence.

When Philip was ready to leave, he said, as a kind of apology, "I'm distracted this morning. It's work."

"Didn't you sleep well?"

"Oh sure, I slept like a log."

"I didn't sleep at all. I'll probably take a nap this morning. So maybe you shouldn't call. I think I need a nap."

He paused and turned to her, questioning.

"Just a nap," she said, and added, "I didn't say pills."

"No. Of course not. I didn't mean. Have a good nap." He kissed her quickly and left.

She watched him go and she was angry. She *ought* to take a pill, it would serve him right. Maybe she would.

The phone rang and it was Beecher Stubbs.

"Oh, what luck to get you in," Beecher said. "Tell me one thing. Tell me you do not have a date for Thanksgiving. Tell me you'll come to us."

"Hi, Beech, how are you?"

"Tell me you'll come to us for dinner."

"We haven't given a thought to Thanksgiving, Beecher. Sure, we'll come to you. We'd love it."

"I'm actually cooking a turkey. Calvin usually does it, you know, at Thanksgiving and Christmas when the kids come home, but I'm doing it this time, my first ever, because the kids aren't coming this year, they're going to France. Everybody is going to France for Thanksgiving. I can't imagine it myself, so we'd like to have you and Philip."

"Well, we'd love it, Beech."

"And I'm having the Kizers too, I've gotten to like her, I feel bad for her."

Maggie laughed. The Kizers and the Tates for Thanksgiving dinner. It was funny in its way.

"What?" Beecher said. "How are you doing, you dear thing?"

"I'm wonderful," Maggie said, "I take it one day at a time."

"We're proud of you," Beecher said. "We love you."

"I know you do," Maggie said. "It means a lot."

She rang off and went upstairs and took a sleeping pill and lay down on her bed. She was trembling with rage. Not a metaphor, she noted, but an unpleasant fact: she was physically shaking with rage. Philip had betrayed her with Dixie Kizer: she felt the betrayal all over again, as if it had just happened.

After a while she got up and poured herself a glass of vodka. It wouldn't smell and it would let her get to sleep. And then she could face the life of terminal clichés: one day at a time, easy does it, let go and let God.

When she woke, it was noon and the room was hot and she was covered in sweat. She took a bath and put on fresh clothes. Her anger was gone, but she was very nervous and she felt that any minute she would burst into tears. She thought of Buck and his Neon Palace, those crazy times; what could she have been thinking? She thought of Dixie and her poor-little-me performance that all the men fell for. Even Beecher Stubbs believed it. Oh, to hell with all of them. She had to be calm. She had to forget her anger at Philip and Dixie and get on with her own life. *Her* life was what mattered here, and she had it back on track, and she was not going to let it go off the tracks now.

She phoned Emma at school, but she was not in her room. She phoned Cole. His flatmate answered and said Cole was in the lab, he's always in the lab. "Just tell him his mother called," she said. "Just to say hello." Who else could she call? Nobody. And so she was alone again, in this house, trapped.

She got down her worn copy of *The Waste Land* and began to read. She couldn't concentrate, but that didn't matter because she knew it almost by heart. The point was to keep occupied, not to think, not to let herself get angry.

But she was angry, and she was not forgiving, and she didn't give fuck-all about any of them. They were not, they were *not* going to drive her to drink.

"No," she said aloud, "I'll drive myself. I've got nobody to blame but myself."

She went into the kitchen and poured herself a vodka and, standing at the sink, she drank it down, straight. Her throat burned, and her lungs, and she began to cough. But after a while the pain subsided and she poured herself another. She took a deep breath. The worst was over.

In her dream the phone was ringing and she kept waiting for Philip to answer it, but Philip was out diddling Dixie Kizer and she would have to answer it herself. She awoke and picked up the phone.

"Hello," she said, her voice groggy.

"Mother? Are you all right? The phone must have rung fifty times."

"Philip isn't home," she said.

"Mother! It's me. Cole. What's going on up there?"

"Hello, Cole," she said. Cole had been such a sweet baby. She lay back on the pillow and shut her eyes. He had been a little lamb.

On the other end of the phone, Cole was silent. She sounded completely drunk. It was bad enough that neither of them had told him about the collapse, the rehab place, the A.A. meetings—he had to hear it all from Dixie Kizer—but this pretense that everything was perfect was just about killing him. How had they ever slipped into this middle-class fantasy of happy families? Everybody nice. Everybody faithful. And meanwhile his mother was drinking herself to death and his father . . . Well, what *was* his father doing?

"Is Father there?" he asked.

"Oh, Cole, you worry too much. Your father is at work and I'm just taking a nap. I didn't sleep last night. Your father snores."

"Mother, you sound . . . bad. You sound as if you've been drinking." He waited. "Have you?"

"I had a little drink. What's so bad about that?"

"Oh, Mother." He thought his heart would break. He repeated the words to himself—my heart will break—and like the dutiful son he was, he felt tears prick at his eyes. Why didn't his father feel this way? Why didn't his father *do* something about this? "Mother, I'm gonna come home." He waited again. "Mother?"

There was only silence on the line.

"Mother?" he said again. "Mother?"

"You do what you have to, darling. That's what we all do anyhow, isn't it." She hung up the phone.

* * *

By the time Philip got home, Maggie had slept soundly, gotten up for more pills and another drink, and was sleeping soundly again.

"Hell-o-o," Philip called as he let himself in. The door was locked, not a good sign. "Hell-o-o," he called again, but it was too late. He had already seen the vodka bottle on the kitchen counter and he knew what that meant. Nevertheless he walked through the downstairs rooms, calling out to her, knowing it was too late—she'd done it again—but, in spite of the evidence, still hoping. He paused at the foot of the stairs. Since her return home, he had lived in constant expectation of trouble. He couldn't help it. During the past year he had gotten into a number of bad habits: checking the liquor bottles, looking in her closet for pills, testing her breath, her walk, the sheen of her eyes. Looking for trouble, always. And here it was, trouble. He was shaking. He rested his head against the banister and said, "Don't let it be. Don't let it." He went upstairs.

Maggie was unconscious, her face white, her brow hot. He took her pulse; it was slow, but acceptable. He moved to the foot of the bed and stood there looking at her. He was hollow in-side, he was bitter, and he was angry. He had tried so hard. *She* had tried so hard. What did you have to do to get through this life—not well, not happily, but just get through it with some kind of decency and dignity and . . . what? Well, he knew the answer. This was fate, this was life, it was what they were stuck with, both of them. But he was not resigned to it.

He fixed her pillows, straightened the sheets, got a cool washcloth and laid it across her brow. He sat beside her on the bed, her hand in his. She looked like a beautiful corpse. The booze, though, had exacted its price. Around her eyes and mouth were thin wrinkles that hadn't been there before. And her jaw-line was going slack. He saw suddenly how she would look in a few years if she kept on drinking. Or even if she didn't. He turned away. He forced himself to think of that moment in the motel when he had found her lying on the floor. He had lain down with her. He had held her in his arms and at that moment he had accepted her forever, however she might be, because he loved her. No conditions. No recriminations. No false hopes. And he would do it again. He took the washcloth from her brow and hung it up in the bathroom. He looked into the mirror. "You poor shit," he said.

He went downstairs and made himself a sandwich, peanut butter and strawberry jam, and he ate it in front of the television. The phone rang but he ignored it. The answering machine took over and he heard Cole's voice, angry, complaining, demanding that *someone* call him immediately. He gave Cole the finger and continued to watch the news. Cole phoned again a half hour later, and again after fifteen minutes. Philip gave in.

"Hello, son," he said.

"Well! At last! Do you mind telling me what's going on?"

"It's nice to hear *your* voice too, son."

"Look, I'm worried. I'm frantic. And I have no idea what's going on up there, Father. Would you mind letting me know, please?"

"Since you ask so nicely, yes. As you know, your mother has had a problem with substance abuse for some time now and a couple months back, in late September, she decided to do something about it. She checked herself in to—"

"Oh Christ, I *know* all about McLean and her leaving you and the apartment in Boston. Dixie told me all about that. I want to know what's going on *now*."

"Dixie told you. Dixie Kizer?"

"Look, I'm coming home. Clearly it's the only way I'm gonna find out what's actually happening there. *Why* did you let this happen?"

"Oh, Cole. If only it were as easy as that."

"I'll be home this week. I'll be home for Thanksgiving."

"Cole, stay there and do your work. There's nothing you can do here that's gonna help."

"Good-bye, Father."

Philip hung up the phone and shook his head. They were great kids, both of them, everybody said so. But sometimes he wondered.

He looked in on Maggie and she was sleeping soundly. There was nothing he could do. He went down and poured himself a stiff scotch.

It was strange to be drinking again. Except at parties, he hadn't had a drink since Maggie's return home and he was surprised at how sharp the scotch tasted and how it smelled, like burned rubber. It did nothing for him. He didn't feel different, not better, not worse.

He finished the drink and tried to watch TV. He flipped through all the channels, and then went through them again, and settled finally on one of the preachers. He didn't know which one it was, but he was funnier than most of them. He had a prettyish face, with black curly hair that looked dyed, and big eyes and very red lips. He was sort of a clerical Kewpie doll. At the moment he was offering peace, of mind and soul, if only you trust in the Lord. "I trust," Philip said aloud. "So how about it?" The preacher suddenly began to babble, and Philip wondered if the TV was malfunctioning, but then the preacher stopped babbling and explained that he had been enraptured, caught up in sacred converse with the Lord, and now he had a message for everybody out there in television land. "Send in your pledges. It can be five dollars or five thousand dollars. Send till it hurts and, sayeth the Lord, it will be given to you a hundredfold. This I promise you, and I"—the camera zoomed in for a frightening close-up—"I am the apple of God's eye."

Philip closed his eyes and slept.

When he woke, it was very dark out. Another preacher was on the TV, also asking for donations, and Philip clicked it off and looked at his watch. It was after midnight.

He went upstairs and looked in on Maggie. She had not moved. She was lying on her back, breathing easily now, and she did not move or respond when he kissed her forehead. He sat with her for a while and then he went downstairs and got in his car and drove.

He followed the route of that first night. He drove to Winchester and swung by the Aspergarters' house and was struck again by how very rich they were. The house, the neighborhood, the low fieldstone walls. The security systems.

This is where it all began, his trouble. He drove around for a while, aimlessly, and then took the cul-de-sac past the Kizers' house. No cars in the drive. No lights anywhere. Hal must be out somewhere buggering a corpse, and Dixie . . . better not even think what Dixie was doing. He drove home.

If Maggie was awake, he would tell her now and be done with it. It was a stupid secret at best but, stupid or not, this was the dark thing that lay at the heart of their problems, he was certain now. It was his secret—not what it was in itself but what it implied—that had caused them to drift apart. It had made him hold back in their sex life. And even though addiction was a mystery of its own, he was sure that his secret somehow explained Maggie's surrender to drugs and to alcohol.

He would tell her. Now.

He went upstairs and found Maggie sitting up in bed, a drink in her hand.

"I have something to tell you," she said.

"No," he said, "let me."

She laughed, a harsh sound. She was very drunk. "I thought I forgave you for the affair with Dixie. But I didn't. I don't." She could barely speak. "Maybe tomorrow or next week or . . .

sometime ... when I'm sober, I'll tell you that I do forgive you, but I don't, Philip, and I never will. I want you to know that."

The glass slipped from her hand and a dark stain spread across the blanket. Philip set about cleaning up the mess.

21

There was every reason why Thanksgiving should be a disaster. Maggie was only in her third day of recovery. Philip was raddled with guilt and anxiety. Neither of them wanted to see the Kizers. For that matter, neither of them wanted to see the Stubbses or anybody else, particularly not their irate son Cole. And on top of all that, Beecher Stubbs would be cooking dinner.

After her startling lapse from sobriety, Maggie had made an amazing recovery. She woke the next morning, headachy and depressed, but she showered and brushed her teeth and asked Philip to join her for a run. They jogged for a short while and then walked for a longer while and then she went home to bed. They didn't talk about what had happened. They didn't talk at all. Philip went off to work and Maggie set the alarm clock in time to attend a noon A.A. meeting with Calvin Stubbs. "It's a matter of getting right back on the horse," Calvin told her, and though she found the image less than helpful, she attended another meeting that night. She worked out on the exercise bike, she jogged, she drank a lot of coffee. By the time Cole arrived home on Wednesday night, she was calm and in control and, in the face of Cole's outrage, she was casually dismissive.

"Would you please explain to me what's been going on!"

They were in the little family room and Cole was confronting them, his back to the TV.

"Cole, Cole," Philip said. "What a tone to take."

"I think I'm owed an explanation."

"We're adults, Cole, with problems of our own. We do the best we can. I don't think we need to be talked to in this way. I won't have it and it upsets your mother."

"Let me explain," Maggie said. "I had a drinking problem— I *have* a drinking problem—and I'm doing something about it. Since it hasn't yet affected your life, Cole, it seems to me that it's none of your business."

"Exactly," Philip said.

"Well, I don't think that if I phone you up and find you're drunk out of your mind, it's none of my business. I think it's very much my business. And I think somebody ought to be in charge around here."

"You?" Maggie said.

"You," Cole said. "Or you."

"Thank you for that," Maggie said. "I'll be in charge if nobody objects. And since I'm in charge, I'd recommend you get some rest tonight, Cole. We're having Thanksgiving dinner with the Stubbses and the Kizers and I know you'll want to be at your best. And now please move from in front of the TV because your father and I would like to watch the eleven o'clock news."

Cole, outraged but silenced, went out to look up friends.

Beecher Stubbs was nearly out of her mind.

"Come in, come in, you dear things," she said. "Oh Calvin, get them drinks, they've got to have drinks. And Cole, what a sweet boy you are to come to an old people's Thanksgiving dinner, and so handsome too, and so tall! I'm cooking it myself, so God knows what it will be like. You know the Kizers, don't you? Cole is an old friend, a young one. He was just a baby. And Dixie has taken up painting again, such a good painter, have you seen? And all you shrinks must promise no shrink-talk tonight. I must go look at my turkey."

Calvin gave them drinks. Only Hal and Cole were having wine. The rest had Perrier with a wedge of lemon, so everybody feared the conversation would be labored. But it took off almost at once, with talk of Tippi Gaspard and how chic she was looking these days and then on to the awfullest films they had seen this past summer and then little groups formed. Hal and Calvin fell into a private discussion of investment banking scandals and how they should have been prevented. Maggie and Cole and Dixie talked about painting, Dixie's painting first, and when that began to make Dixie nervous, she switched the conversation to painters their rich friends collected. Klee and Mondrian and McKnight. The Aspergarters, she heard, had bought a Kandinsky, or maybe they just had it on loan. The McGuinns were hoping to buy . . . Philip, who had been helping Beecher in the kitchen, called them all to the table.

Calvin carved while everybody said nice things about the beautiful roasted color of the turkey and the wonderful smell and how you needed a turkey for Thanksgiving or it just wasn't Thanksgiving, but then it appeared that the turkey wasn't, in fact, cooked. Calvin attacked a leg and it would not give. He could not cut through it nor could he wrench it off. It began to bleed at the joint. "Oh dear," he said, and the leg flopped back and forth, bloody and still attached. He went to work on the breast. The first slice came off smooth and beautiful and there was a sigh of relief around the table. But the second slice resisted and as Calvin pressed down, juice began to rise along the back of the knife and the juice was red. Everybody was watching. "Oh dear," he said again. "It'll have to go back to the oven." "But my dressing," Beecher said, "and all my nice veggies," and everybody said not to worry, they could eat the veggies first and have the turkey afterward. "Like in France,"

Beecher said. "What a good idea since everybody is in France
this Thanksgiving anyway." So Calvin spooned out the dressing and Beecher passed her veggies and everybody ate, but not
very much. The dressing—oyster and prune—looked positively
scary and the vegetables, they found, were underdone. The baby
potatoes were like white stones, and the turnip and carrots were
like colored stones, and the peas were like tiny perfect green
stones. They ate a lot of celery and radishes and pushed the
colored stones around their plates. Conversation slowed and
then stopped. Everyone was nervous. And then suddenly Philip
began to laugh. They were little abrupt laughs, like coughs, but
they went on for some time until finally he stopped and shook
his head, sadly.

"This is really awful, Beecher," he said, his voice warm and
sincere. "This is your worst ever."

There was silence for perhaps a second and then Beecher
began to laugh, and the others, relieved, began to laugh as well.
Maggie was delighted and she said softly, "How funny, how
funny," but she was thinking, I love you, I love you, and it was
like old times and, for that minute, she was very happy.

"It *is* terrible," Beecher said. "I've quite outdone myself."
Then everyone tried to top everyone else, saying how awful the
meal was, how stony and inedible, until it was time for the turkey again, but nobody could stand it. Beecher cried a little bit—
she couldn't help it, she said, all that *work* and just for a good
laugh—but then she brought out dessert, which she'd bought
at the Winchester Bakery. There was a pumpkin pie and a mince
and a lemon meringue and they devoured all three. It was a very
funny Thanksgiving dinner.

Maggie and Philip were getting ready for bed. She looked up
from brushing her teeth and said, through the foam, "That meal!"

"It was very funny, wasn't it."

"*You* were very funny. You were outrageous. It was like old times."

Philip was getting into his pajamas and paused to think about what she had said.

"And Hal didn't attack Dixie," Maggie said, "as he always seems to do. She was different tonight." She began brushing her hair, hard. "Somehow she doesn't seem so attackable these days. At least not tonight. She seemed very independent, flirtatious almost." She paused in her brushing. "She certainly was flirtatious with Cole, I thought."

"Alas."

"Alas?"

"That phone call he got tonight just after we came in? And then he went out?"

"Not Dixie, surely."

"It's what I suspect. It's what I fear."

"Oh, it couldn't be. Cole? Going after Dixie Kizer? My God!" She said it with contempt and then, realizing, she said to Philip, "Sorry 'bout that."

They thought.

"No," Maggie said finally, "he's too sane for that. Of course he *is* mad for sex."

Philip looked at her. "Cole? Mad for sex?"

"My God, he's always been mad for sex. Where have you been? Since high school, maybe even earlier. You didn't know?"

"I begin to think I don't know anything."

She put down her brush and leaned into the mirror to examine the lines at her eyes and mouth. "Sweet Philip," she said. "Innocent Philip." She was being mean and enjoying it but suddenly she felt hollow inside. She turned to face him. "You know the things I said when I was drunk?"

Philip listened.

"That I'd never forgive you? That I'd never love you?"

"You didn't say you'd never love me."

"Well, I thought it."

"Don't, Maggie."

"Well, I want you to know that it's not always *in vino veritas*. I said those things to hurt you, only. Not because they were true, but because they would hurt you."

"I know."

"I wanted to hurt you. I wanted to *really* hurt you."

"Well, you did."

They waited, both of them.

"I do forgive you," she said.

"And do you love me?"

"I forgive you. We'll have to start with that."

They got into bed and for a long time they lay there awake.

Maggie fell asleep finally and dreamed of the terrible Thanksgiving dinner. But in the dream she was calling out to him across a great table, and the table grew wider and longer as she called, and he was so distant he could not hear her as again and again she begged him, "Forgive me, forgive me."

22

Maggie began to write down her dreams.

She got a black and white notebook with green paper, the kind she had used in grammar school. It had a sewn binding, so you couldn't get rid of what you wrote except by tearing it out. You had to live with everything you put on paper.

She wrote down her Thanksgiving dream, which embarrassed her a lot, but she wrote it down anyway. And then she wrote down other dreams, repeated ones she had had as a girl, and later in college, and then she wrote not about dreams but about things as they were. She wrote about Philip and about herself and about what had happened to them. She wrote as if she were preparing a document for Leona Spitzer, hard facts, concrete incidents, but it didn't help and she didn't go to see Leona Spitzer. She made up things, to see if she could get closer to the truth by distorting the facts. She made Philip a pure villain and then she made herself the villain and then she gave up on villains.

"I forgive him," she wrote, "even though he has betrayed me with another woman." And then she wrote, "But is that true, any of it? That I forgive him? That he betrayed me?"

And she wrote, "You're a cold woman and you're proud of it."

And she wrote, "I'm afraid for you."

And she wrote, "Why did I dream that I was begging his forgiveness?"

She wrote a kind of story about the times Philip had made her laugh. They were scenes from reality, but she made up lines for people to say and things for them to do and she drew neat moral conclusions which really didn't fit the scenes.

She read Virginia Woolf and found she was no help at all.

She wrote a story called "The Great Thanksgiving Dinner" in which she tried to catch Philip's wonderful outrageousness. He'd been like that—crazy and outrageous, saying any old thing—when they'd first met at college, and she'd fallen in love with him on account of it. But she couldn't get the story right. She was tempted to tear it out, but not getting things right was part of what she had to live with, and so she kept it.

She read Faulkner and Hemingway and Fitzgerald. She read Dickens and Thackeray. They were even less help than Virginia Woolf.

She wrote a poem which was very bad.

She read *Pride and Prejudice* and then she read all of Jane Austen in the order of composition and she had a very good time. Jane Austen knew all about life. She wondered briefly if Jane Austen had had a drinking problem. A drop too much sherry? Jane Austen knew about love. Did she? And forgiveness?

She wrote down all the things she wanted in a man and was surprised to find she was describing Philip. The other things, the things he did not have, didn't really matter to her.

"He is loving," she wrote, "he is lovable." She must tell him this. Sometime.

She wrote down a list of her faults: the things she had done and the things she had left undone. Could she really be nothing and yet guilty of so much? Wasn't the humility negated by the arrogance?

She began to forgive herself. She felt less cold already.

The point is, she wrote, does he forgive me? She resisted underlining he and me, though she had taken the point.

She watched him, waiting for him to confront her. He didn't, though. You wouldn't either, she thought, if you were married to me. To think this was very funny. She wrote it down. You wouldn't either if you were married to me. She knew she was getting better.

She was tired of confronting herself.

Poor Bartleby, she wrote.

On a hard gray day in late November she burned the notebook. It had done its job. She stood by the grill in the backyard and watched the pages curl, browning from the outer edges, and was surprised that she felt nothing except a curious, dull satisfaction. She poked the pages apart to help them burn and she let herself get lost, not in thought, but in the act of burning. All that time, all that misery, gone.

Snow began to fall, slowly, softly, but she pulled her jacket tight around her and waited until the last of the flames died away. Then she went into the house and, uncertain why, she looked out the window. In just this little time the world outside had begun to turn white.

23

Long before January 1 the news got out that Philip Tate was to be the new Dean of the Medical School. He refused interviews until after his official appointment, but the local newspapers ran stories about him anyway. There were articles about his distinguished career, about his father's distinguished career, about his son in Johns Hopkins Medical and his daughter at Berkeley—both outstanding students who would certainly have distinguished careers—and about Philip's wife Maggie, who had sacrificed her career as a scholar, they said, to support her husband through medical school. Maggie Tate, a leader in the community, taught Freshman Composition at a local college. They did not say which one.

At the medical school, things went on as usual. New deans had been appointed before this and they'd be appointed again in the future and Philip Tate was, all things considered, a smart psychiatrist and your basic good guy. Nobody minded his being Dean.

There were the customary round of Christmas parties and Hanukkah parties and, this year, small dinner parties for Philip and Maggie. Maggie had dreaded these, and so had Philip, but they carried them off with increasing ease. Maggie was her old self, except she didn't drink. She was warm and witty and personable; she seemed happy for Philip. He, however, was more reticent than usual. He turned attention on Maggie whenever he could, he was self-deprecatory, he seemed to have some new modesty—almost shyness—about him. If he was not himself, it was because he was even nicer: this was how their friends reported the situation to one another and it was how Dixie Kizer reported it to Cole. "He's a new man, your father," she said on the phone, "and your mother, of course, is an inspiration."

Christmas came, and the kids arrived for the holidays, and Emma brought with her a friend from Greece, Katina Apostolides. They were in love, Emma explained, they were lesbians, so everybody better get used to it. Philip smiled narrowly and said nothing, but Maggie welcomed the two girls and took them up to Emma's room, chatting and laughing as if it were not the end of the world. She left them to get settled in, or to do whatever unthinkable things they intended to do, and she came downstairs to console Philip.

"She's done with men," Maggie said. "Men are pigs now. Men are swine." She laughed softly.

"*How* can you find any of this funny? This is crazy. This is insane."

"It's not insane."

"Our own daughter comes home and tells us she's a lesbian and brings her lover with her and they're upstairs *doing* it in our own house? And that's not insane?"

"She's still Emma. It's a phase."

Philip was silent for a while and then he said, "What happened to the Professor? That Bubba."

"Bubby, not Bubba. Bubby turned out to be a . . . a dork, I believe."

"A dork?"

"Bubby's a dork and Katina is her lover. But keep in mind that Katina is a senior this year, so the lesbian stuff may be all over by June."

"I can't bear it."

She put her arms around him and held him to her. "Of course you can bear it," she said. "You just don't like it. But you can bear it."

"Oh God," he said, "what would I do without you."

"Keep it in mind," she said. "Cole gets here tomorrow."

Cole arrived anxious and exhausted but he had gained a good ten pounds and was looking handsomer than ever.

"My gorgeous son," Maggie said. "Just look at you."

They all looked at him, including Katina, who looked too long and too admiringly, Emma thought, and so she said, "He's just another male, Katina, another oppressor." Katina said nothing, but she did those flirty things with her eyes, and Emma took her out at once to show her the town.

"So what's this with Emma and her friend?" Cole asked. "Is this what I think?"

"They're lesbians, quote, and we'd all quote better get used to it," Maggie said.

"I can't bear it," Philip said.

"It's a phase," Cole said. "It doesn't mean anything."

"You see?" Maggie said.

"Of course, it might be for real," Cole said. "You have to find these things out. You have to experiment."

"Which brings to mind your apartment mate, Cole," Philip said. "Is he or isn't he?"

Cole looked at him.

"Is he just a roommate?" Philip had decided it was time to find out these things.

"Is he gay, you mean?"

"Is he your lover, I mean."

Cole laughed. "You've gotta be joking," he said. "You're out of touch, Father."

His father was out of touch, Cole had always known that, and his mother, when she drank, was considerably more than out of touch. But he could see, even from the brief time he'd been home, that things were better between them, which lifted a huge responsibility from his shoulders. He went upstairs to sleep, saying, over his shoulder, "You're cute, the two of you."

"Our kids," Philip said. "I can't bear it."

"They love you," she said. "Me too."

He hugged her, pleased, though he was uncertain what she meant.

New Year's Eve was rainy and messy. It had snowed all day, but toward evening the snow had turned to rain.

Philip and Maggie had planned their usual open house, with all their Medical School friends and Maggie's college friends and the two kids, of course, and all their friends, but this year, since it was the night of Philip's official appointment as Dean, the party seemed larger or more important or more something.

"More frantic," Philip said. "At least the preparations are."

"Everything's prepared," Maggie said, "if only the rain lets up."

The preparations lasted the entire day. They had begun early that morning when Kappy's Liquors delivered the drinks. There was a case of wine and a case of beer, and a mixed case of scotch and bourbon and gin, and this year, for the first time, there was Perrier and Pellegrino and Calistoga water, plain and flavored, fizzy and regular, and a case of Coke. In the afternoon Schaub's showed up, early, with a turkey and a ham and a loin of pork. These were cooked, of course, and elaborately decorated, and enshrined on fake silver platters that took up lots of room. "But where do they *go*?" Maggie said. "Where do I *put* them?" and she emptied the refrigerator of everything that wouldn't spoil. At eight, on schedule, Ollie's Catering delivered the hors d'oeuvres, the two bartenders arrived along with the two serving men, and everything was set to begin.

Maggie, in the living room, adjusted her earrings. She had on a new cocktail dress, white, shot with silver, and her hair looked good and—she took a deep breath—she was, as much as she would ever be, ready. Philip came down the stairs, ready as well.

"Now," Maggie said, "if only the damned rain would stop."

"Fuck the rain," Philip said. "I'm gonna have a Pellegrino." He gave her a kiss and they waited.

The rain stopped at nine, just as the guests began to arrive. The Stubbses were first and then came the old-timers, the Gaspards and the Aspergarters, and then a whole mass of people arrived, and suddenly it was a party, with lots of noise, and someone playing the piano in the family room, and, blessedly, laughter.

Around eleven the young people arrived in a large group. They were noisier and they drank more and in no time there was a lot of smoke in the air and a feeling of excitement. With so many good-looking people, talented and sexy and popular, nearly everybody felt lucky to be there.

"It's a real party," Maggie said.

"It's a good party," Philip said, "thanks to you. It's *all* thanks to you." They were alone in the kitchen, and he drew her gently close and kissed her, and then he kissed her with passion. She responded—all those awful months seemed to fall away—and she pressed herself against him. They held each other for a long time.

"Sorry to interrupt."

They separated and turned toward the door, where Hal Kizer was standing, an odd smile on his face.

"That's very nice," Hal said.

He said, "Really nice."

And he said, "Surprising, really."

"Happy New Year," Maggie said.

"Sorry to interrupt, as I say, but I'm gonna be leaving now and I wanted to thank you for the party and congratulate you on being Dean."

"It's not midnight," Philip said. "Surely you're gonna stay till midnight."

"Got a hot date," Hal said, "downtown."

"It can wait," Maggie said. "Think of Dixie for once."

"Oh, I've invited Dixie, but she says no. I'm on my own."

"Well, be on your own *here*, with us," Maggie said. "It's not a night for driving anyway. It's getting colder and the streets are going to slick over."

"Very dangerous driving," Philip said.

"Come on," Maggie said, "come with me," and put her arm around Hal's waist and led him into the dining room, where Beecher Stubbs was fussing about the dessert table. "Beecher," she said, "talk to poor old Hal, he's on his own." And Maggie drifted away.

"On your own?" Beecher said. "But I just saw Dixie, looking very beautiful, I must say, in red. So how are you on your own? In what sense, I mean?" Before he could answer, she went on. "How is it that you're nice to Dixie when you're alone but so mean to her when you're in public? I'm not the first to notice it. Everybody has noticed it, it's most remarkable, and it makes you look like a very nasty man, but Dixie says you aren't. She says you can be very nice. You call her mousie and you say sweet things."

"How do you know I'm not a very nasty man, period? Despite what Dixie tells you."

"Oh, you mean the kinky-sex thing. That's just psychosis. I discounted that as soon as I was sure you didn't hurt Dixie. I don't count that at all. It has nothing to do with who you are, for real, in real life. Don't you agree?"

Hal smiled. Beecher Stubbs was dangerous, yes, but it was a pleasant surprise to discover she was smart as well.

"Yes?"

"Yes, I agree," he said.

"Well, why aren't you sweet to her in public?"

He thought for a while. He wanted to be honest with this fat, peculiar woman. "I don't know," he said. "I could try to be. I think I will try to be."

"A New Year's resolution," Beecher said. "How nice."

"I'll try right now," he said. He gave Beecher a kiss on the cheek, wished her happy New Year, and moved off to find Dixie.

He found her in the big family room with Cole and Emma and a bunch of their noisy young friends.

"I've come to say nice things to you," Hal said. "It's my New Year's resolution."

"I thought you were leaving," Dixie said.

"I was. I stayed at Beecher's request. To be sweet to you . . . in public."

She looked at him and laughed.

"You're looking very nice." He whispered, "Very sexy."

"I thought you were going."

"Do you *want* me to go?"

"I'll tell you a secret." She leaned close and whispered in his ear, "I want you dead."

He pulled back and looked at her. She'd been drinking. This kind of thing happened when she drank. It didn't matter. He would try again.

"How about a New Year's kiss?" he said.

She touched her lips to his and he could smell the liquor on her breath. She moved closer to whisper in his ear again. But she did not whisper. She said, loudly, "Go fuck yourself."

Hal turned from her and left the Tates' party and set off for Boston to keep his date with Theda. It was turning cold and the roads were slick.

The Tates' party continued on without him. Suddenly, from the little TV room, there came a cheer and the sound of horns blowing and cries of "Happy New Year!" that spread through the house as everybody began kissing and shaking hands and wishing all best to each other.

"Everybody, everybody," Aspergarter called out. He banged on a glass and shouted "Everybody!" until he got their attention. In the other rooms, people began shushing one another. "Ah," he said, "sweet silence." Nobody laughed. He raised his voice, a proclamation: "Join me, everybody, in welcoming our new Dean to his new job. Hip hip!" And they actually responded, "Hooray!" So he did it twice more until general laughter broke out, and then conversation, and after a while the older ones began to drift off toward home. It was the New Year.

Emma, who had drunk several glasses of wine, kissed her mother and began to cry. "I'm so proud of you," she said. "You too, Daddy," and she flung her arms around him. Katina stood beside her looking embarrassed. "Kat and I are going out now with the others, but I just want you to know, I think you're the two most wonderful, most supportive, most understanding parents in the world." She kissed them both again and ran from the room. Katina smiled shyly and followed Emma out.

Almost at once Cole appeared and shook his father's hand. "Father," he said, "congratulations. Mother, we're very proud of you, Emma and I."

"Cole," Maggie said.

"Son," Philip said.

Cole kissed each of them in turn, solemnly, and left.

"Well, they *are* great kids," Philip said.

"Everyone knows that," Maggie said. "We're lucky. That's all there is to it. We're lucky."

All the young people left in a group—to party on, they said—and Dixie Kizer left along with them, and pretty soon the Tates' party was over. The Stubbses were the last to go, thanking Maggie and congratulating Philip and apologizing yet again for the unspeakable Thanksgiving dinner. And then it was just Maggie and Philip and the cleaning people. In an hour more the cleaning people had gone.

Maggie and Philip, happy, relieved, went upstairs to bed.

* * *

The roads were very slick and they hadn't been sanded yet, so Hal had to drive slowly. Originally, when he'd made the date with Theda, he had thought what a great idea it would be to have her do her British trick—with the orange slice in the mouth and the toe-wire controlling the action—so that as the bells rang in the New Year, he'd ring his own bells and come like fucking Vesuvius. It was silly, he knew that, but he had daydreamed about it all during the holidays. He could have had it, too, if he hadn't let himself be sidetracked by Beecher Stubbs and then tried to be nice to Dixie.

He was still smarting from Dixie's betrayal, in public no less, dismissing him in front of all those young kids. She had actually told him to go fuck himself. They were polite kids so they pretended it was all a joke and everybody had laughed and somebody had even punched him on the arm, a good-guy gesture, but the fact was she had betrayed him. Humiliated him. He stepped on the gas and the car skidded and leaped forward. Thank God for the Mercedes. At least he had something reliable in his life.

Theda's place was on Commonwealth Avenue, an old town house divided into apartments for computer programmers and teachers and retirees on a fixed pension. And Theda. As usual there was no place to park. He smacked the steering wheel with his open palm and then, resigned, drove around the block, once, and then a second time. Finally he said to hell with it and parked next to a hydrant with the front end of his car partially blocking a private driveway. It was getting very cold. He walked carefully down the street to her building. The sidewalk was iced over and treacherous, so he stepped aside and walked in the snow. The slush spilled over into his shoes.

In the outside lobby he pressed Theda's buzzer, 4-B, but there was no answering buzz. He knew she was home and he knew nobody else was there because he paid her extremely well and she was not about to jeopardize such a good steady income. Besides, she hadn't yet gotten her Christmas bonus. He pressed the buzzer again. He went out to the street and looked up to the fourth floor. There were lights on up there, but that didn't prove anything since her apartment was in the rear. He went back to the lobby and buzzed her again.

He tried buzzing 4-A. No response. He began to buzz randomly, hitting each of the buttons in succession, but there was no response from any of them. He pressed 4-A again, and at once there was a voice on the intercom, a very sleepy voice.

"Who's that?"

Surprised, he did not know what to say and he blurted out, "It's Hal."

"Hal?"

"Right."

"Who the fuck is Hal?"

"I'm buzzing for Theda. In 4-B."

"She's not here."

"I know that. She's in 4-B. I want to go to 4-B." He was shouting. He felt like a fool.

"She's not there, I'm telling you."

"She is there."

"Go fuck yourself, Charlie," he said, but he pressed the door-release button and Hal was inside at last.

Upstairs, on the door of 4-B, there was a note in Theda's handwriting. "Mother ill. Home sometime in January." And she signed it with a little heart.

Hal went slowly down the stairs and stood on the sidewalk next to his car. He looked up and down the street and then at his watch: 1 A.M. His shoes were soaking wet. Happy New Year. He had other numbers he could call, but they'd be booked tonight for sure and besides he had his heart set on the British thing. He tugged at his crotch. Very nice. Very ready. He could drive around and pick up a likely hooker. It would be better than nothing.

He got in his car and drove down Commonwealth to the Public Garden and then cruised lower Marlborough Street. The streets here had been sanded and there was a surprising amount of action—and cop cars too, he noticed—but mostly it was just gays on the prowl. And then he saw a hot little number in black stretch pants and three-inch heels and a metal-studded top. She was a caricature of what he was looking for but, let's face it, he was desperate. She was black, with long blond hair and fantastic boobs, and against his better judgment, Hal pulled in ahead of her and stopped the car. She approached on the driver's side and leaned in the window. "Hi, porky, how they hanging?" she said. The voice was deep and the face was unmistakably a man's. Hal stepped on the gas and the car pulled away, but not before she planted a solid kick in the rear fender. "Racist!" she hollered.

Hal took Storrow Drive and headed for home.

The roads were a mess and he drove slowly. He was shaken, he realized, by his reaction to the fact that the hooker was a man. From a little distance he could have sworn it was a woman— great legs, a great ass—and he wondered now why he had been so put off. What difference, finally, would it have made? He thought about this. Was he homophobic? No. No, he was as tolerant as the next guy. He thought some more. Look, he just didn't want any man fiddling around between his legs, period. In sex there were certain proprieties that had to be observed. That's just how it was. And he didn't want to think about it any longer. Anyway he was almost home.

As he left Route 93 and pulled onto West Border Road, there was a banging in the engine and the car began to shake. "Shit," Hal said aloud, and hit the brakes. The car began to slow and then suddenly struck a patch of ice and fishtailed wildly to the right. Hal corrected with a sharp pull to the left and then had to recorrect with a pull to the right. The car seemed to elevate, completely out of control, as it spun around in a perfect circle. And then, miraculously, it hit a patch of gravel. Hal was able to ease down on the brake and come to a shaky stop. He pulled to the side of the road and turned off the ignition. His heart was racing. He was covered with sweat. He'd been frightened, he realized, not a good feeling and not a good way to begin the New Year. He sat there a moment, breathing deeply, and then he started the car. There was a terrific knocking in the engine and the car began to shake. He turned off the ignition.

Out of nowhere a Winchester patrol car pulled up behind him. Two cops. He could see one calling in his license plate while the other one approached his car. He lowered his window.

"I saw you having trouble there. You all right?"

"I guess. I don't know. Let me start it up and see."

"Hold on. Hold on. You been celebrating a little tonight, sir? You have anything to drink?" He leaned into the car.

"A glass of wine, hours ago."

"That's good, that's good. The life you save may be your own, as they like to say. Can I see your driver's license, sir?" And as Hal got out his license and registration, the cop looked up at the sky. "Lovely evening now the rain has stopped. Slippery, though. I'll be just a moment, sir." He took the license and registration and walked to the patrol car. After a moment he returned. "Everything seems in good order, sir." But he continued to examine the license and registration. "Coming back from a trip?"

"Yes, as a matter of fact."

"And where was that, sir?"

"Just Boston. Visiting friends. It's the holidays, right?"

"Uh-huh, very nice."

He continued to examine the license.

Psychologically, it was a very interesting routine: intimidation by politeness.

The cop handed over the registration, glanced at the license one more time, and handed that over too.

"Well, you're almost home. Woodlawn Drive. Very nice area. Start the car, why don't you, and see if it's still giving you trouble."

Hal started the car and it made a grinding sound, and then there was a knocking in the engine, but he edged it forward a few feet.

"I think I can make it home."

"Sounds to me like the water pump. We'll follow along, make sure you're okay." He walked back to the patrol car. "Happy New Year!" he called.

"Yeah, sure," Hal said.

It was only a few minutes' drive to Woodlawn, but he could see he wasn't going to make it. He pulled into the first service station he came to. They were closed, except for gas, but he left the car with the old man there and said he'd come by and explain in the morning. He fingered the small round dent in the rear fender—the perfect shape of a stiletto heel. The police pulled in behind him and offered to drive him home, but he said no, he needed the air, he wanted to walk, he needed to clear his head.

"On these streets? I don't think so."

They drove him home.

"Happy New Year," they said, and laughed, as he got out of the car.

He walked up the drive to the back door. His feet were soaking, his shoes were ruined, and he was going to come down with a cold. Some year to look forward to. And all because of his stupid dick. He tugged at it and it responded, old faithful. He let himself in and sat down to rest. Dixie wasn't there, but he hadn't really expected her. She was still out with those kids, drinking and telling jokes and smoking grass, he supposed, and maybe laughing at him. How could she have done that? How could she have betrayed him like that in public? Well, fuck her. He was exhausted. He was dead tired.

"I'm dead," he said aloud to the empty kitchen. "I'm a dead man."

But he was wrong. He would not be dead until nearly 3 A.M.

Cole and his crowd were having a terrific time despite the rain. They had gone from Dante's Inferno to the Oasis to Buck's Neon Palace, with a drink at each bar, and everybody wanted still more partying. It was a great night. The older ones, college and grad school kids, had been through the high stage of their drinking and the rowdy stage and they were getting on toward the romantic stage. Emma and Katina had long since reached the romantic stage. For some time now they'd been going from place to place snuggling cozily and doing kissy-kissy, but nobody seemed to mind because, as Dixie Kizer kept saying, they looked just so cute. Cole figured the party would be breaking up soon.

Dixie Kizer had attached herself to Cole from the start. Embarrassed at first—Dixie was married, after all—Cole very soon began to feel good about the situation: a gorgeous older woman on his arm, sexy and experienced, and clearly mad for his body; what more could you ask? They made out, lightly, at the bars and more heavily afterward as they drove from place to place. Cole was feeling very good.

There came a moment, though, when Cole realized he was no longer in charge—Dixie was making the moves—and suddenly he wanted out.

"Listen," he said, "there's something I've gotta get clear."

He was driving her MG, concentrating hard, because he wanted this break to be easy and clean. Her hand moved lightly on his thigh.

"I've got to tell you something, Dixie. This has been a lot of fun and I've been having a really great time, we both have, I think, but, you know, I'm Catholic. What I mean is . . . what we've been doing is a sin, first of all. And then there's the real thing: I'm not ready to make a commitment—my medical career has to come before everything else, *everything*—and you're somebody who deserves a commitment. But I'd really like us to be friends. Okay? I mean, we agreed at the beginning that there were no strings, that we were just in it for some good times, remember? I'm saying this because I don't want you to think later that I've just been leading you on."

She put her hand up between his legs.

"Dixie, have you been listening?"

"Yes," she said, but she did not remove her hand.

Hal lay on the bedroom floor with all his sex paraphernalia. He had found picture wire in the cellar and he had rigged up a kind of noose around his genitals and he'd run the wire down to his big toe, and he had another wire that went from his neck to his toe, and he had the plastic bag almost but not quite over his head, and he had the wedge of orange soaked with amyl nitrate resting on his chest, and he was ready to begin. He wished he had Theda and her magic fingers here to start him off. But he reached down and touched himself and instantly he realized he didn't need Theda. He was hard as hell. He was like a steel spike. He pressed his toe down and the noose tightened and, involuntarily, his back arched off the floor and he felt as if he were being lifted into the air by his dick. He rested a second, caught his breath, and said, "Happy New Year." Then he inserted the orange wedge in his mouth, pulled the bag loosely over his head, and tucked the edges underneath the wire. His brain reeled. He had used a lot of amyl nitrate. He had to rest a minute.

His brain began slowly to return to normal.

Dixie could be part of all this if she would just loosen up. He was angry and hurt at her betrayal. How could she have done it? And then gone off with those kids. She had become a different person. It had begun with her obsession with Philip Tate, following him around like a lunatic, spying on him. Sleeping downstairs. Giving up drinking. She had become another person. He didn't know her anymore. He wondered, had he ever known her? Certainly she had never known him.

He was back in the world suddenly. He realized he was lying on the bedroom floor with wires around his neck, et cetera, and his erection was softening up, and he was about to return to reality altogether.

He bit into the orange wedge; he bore down with his toe. At once his head flopped back and banged against the floor and again he had the sensation of being lifted into the air. His brain spun out somewhere, dazzled.

He did it again. And again.

The lack of oxygen was making everything bright and sweet and happy. It was a phenomenon he knew all about but had never fully experienced. He was in that long tunnel talked about by near-death survivors, a dark passageway with light at the end, and music, and a sense of peace and longing. Time had stopped and he stood on the rim of eternity.

In fact, in scientific fact, it meant nothing. Those near-death idiots thought they saw a vision of an afterlife, when in fact it was only the scrambling of sense data by the misfiring of neurons in a brain deprived of oxygen. There was no end to human folly. Look at Dixie, for instance.

He wished suddenly, passionately, that Dixie were here with him.

And there she was.

He caught a glimpse of her in the light, for just a second, and then she disappeared. He called out to her but she was gone. And then he realized what he must do. He bore down hard with his toe, and he could see her again, and he said, "Look at this, look at me, look," and he felt himself hauled into the air, he was floating, he was adrift on waves of light, and it was good. He was drifting toward her and, just as in the near-death accounts, she was beckoning to him. He bore down harder with his toe. "Yes," he said, "this is what I've always wanted, this is it, yes, this is it." And still she beckoned to him.

Suddenly he was there. They were face-to-face and she was saying something but he could not hear it. "What?" he said, and "What?" He took a deep breath and the air was like incense and he heard her finally. She said, "It's all right. I know you and it's still all right." So he was known at last, and loved for it, and it was wonderful, wonderful. She opened the door and held it for him and he stepped inside. It was pure ecstasy. It was everything he'd hoped for.

"Come on in," Dixie said. She nuzzled him and put one finger inside his belt. Just a tiny tease.

"Oh Dix!" he said. "You're a very wicked girl."

"Just for a little drink," she said. "Nothing more, I promise."

"Yeah, sure. You promise."

"But you want to. You know you do. Just a little bit?" She wiggled her finger inside his belt. "Just a little teeny tiny bit?"

"But what about Hal?"

"Hal won't be home until tomorrow at the earliest. Just a teeny tiny? For Dixie and Cole? No strings attached."

So they went inside the house and Dixie made him a drink and gave him a quick kiss and then dashed upstairs to get into something easier to get out of.

Downstairs Cole sipped his drink and said to himself, This is mad, this is insane, I ought to get out of here before it's too late, because pretty soon it's gonna be too late, but one quick fuck, what harm could it do? And then for no particular reason he stood up, ready to go. "I'm out of here," he said, put down the drink, and made for the front door.

Dixie appeared then, very pale in a green satin dressing gown. She put her hand on Cole's arm and said softly, "Go upstairs. You'd better go upstairs."

"No, I can't," he said. "I've got to go home, Dixie, really." He leaned over to give her a kiss.

She pushed him away, with force, and said, "Go upstairs, you idiot, we've got a problem." She laughed, a short high bark, frightening. "I think he's dead." And as Cole took the stairs three at a time, she shouted after him, "I wanted him dead."

She went into the sunroom and sat on the chaise longue and tried to drink from Cole's glass. But her hand was trembling and the drink spilled and she began to cry, softly at first, and then more loudly, and then like a crazy person. She recognized this scene. It had all happened before, long before, and it was happening again.

Upstairs Cole telephoned his father and when Philip answered, Cole said, "You'd better come here, Father, now. I'm in serious trouble."

"You can't do this," Maggie said, "it'll be the end of your career."

"He's my son," Philip said, and got his coat. "He's our son."

She saw him then as she had tried to see him all those months with her notebook and her reading and her dreams. She saw him clearly.

"Do you forgive me?" she said, and he said, "Yes, of course," and she said, "No, I mean for everything, for all those things, for . . ."

He held her close and kissed her. "Yes," he said, "I forgive you," and he drove to the Kizers' house, full of joy and terror and what had to be, for the lack of a better name, love.

* * *

Philip did the only thing he could do. He lied.

When the police arrived, he met them at the door. "Up-stairs," he said, "in the master bedroom. It's a suicide, I think." The police glanced into the sunroom, where Dixie was still cry-ing hysterically, and then jogged on up the stairs. At once Philip turned to the telephone and called Calvin Stubbs. He was needed immediately, Philip said; come at once to the Kizers' house. Calvin arrived in just a few minutes. "Hal's dead," Philip said, "that's all I can say. Look after Dixie, would you? She's losing it, and this is not the time for her to lose it." Calvin went into the sunroom and sat with Dixie. In a moment he came out and said to Philip, "I'm gonna give her some Nembutal. She's hys-terical." "Yes, yes," Philip said, "do whatever you want." Calvin looked at him strangely and went back to Dixie.

Philip stood in the foyer, waiting.

The police were a long time upstairs, and before they came down other police arrived, two detectives and a lieutenant, and after a while a medical examiner. Philip, waiting at the foot of the stairs, could hear the exclamations of surprise, some sup-pressed laughter, a lot of mumbled conversation. Dixie was stretched out in the sunroom, crying quietly now.

The lieutenant came down the stairs. "Holy shit," he said, and shook his head.

"Yes," Philip said.

"Who found the body?"

"She did. His wife. Mrs. Kizer."

"And you were with her?"

"No, I was down here in the sunroom, over there." He pointed.

"Anybody else here at the time?"

"No. Just she and I."

"You didn't know he was upstairs, dead?"

"Good God, no!"

"But she knew."

"No, it wasn't like that at all. Neither of us knew. We had an open house, at my house, my wife and I, and I was driving Mrs. Kizer home afterward, is all."

"So you dropped her off and went home."

"Yes. No. I stayed for a drink."

"I see. And she went upstairs to slip into something more comfortable?"

"No, that wasn't it at all. She went upstairs to use the bathroom."

"There's no bathroom down here she could have used? In a house this size?" The lieutenant looked at him, interested, but Philip said nothing. "Just asking," the lieutenant said. "Not implying anything. Necessarily."

"She found the body," Philip said. "He was already dead."

"And she called you and you came up the stairs and examined the body."

"I didn't examine the body. I called you. I called the police."

"But you said he was dead. How did you know he was dead if you didn't examine the body?"

"I didn't examine the body in any technical sense. I just checked to make sure he was dead."

"To make *sure* he was dead."

"Well, not like that. I could see he looked dead. He was probably dead. I checked to see if there was anything I could do to revive him. But it was perfectly clear he was dead."

"And in a very unusual way too, you might say."

"Yes."

"They teach you that at medical school? That elegant variation stuff?"

"Dr. Kizer, it appears, had strange sexual . . . appetites. I don't think he's typical of all doctors."

"You might say. The orange in the mouth, the bag over the head. It's like that M.P. in England."

"I don't know anything about that."

"It was in all the papers. He was wearing lady's panty hose or a bra or something like that. It was in the papers."

"Would you please . . . would you not talk so loudly."

"Sorry. It's just that there are easier ways to kill yourself."

"I would imagine it was an unintentional suicide."

"All suicides are, in the final analysis."

"I'm not sure of that."

"I'll want to talk to you later, Dr. Tate. I'm gonna talk to the widow now."

"I think you should wait. I think you should ask her psychiatrist."

"We'll see," the lieutenant said, and crossed to the sunroom. "Mrs. Kizer? I need to talk to you for a few minutes?" He leaned over her, concerned. "Sorry about your loss."

"I did it," Dixie said. She sat upright on the chaise longue, and in a dreamy voice, singsong almost, said, "I wanted him dead. I killed him. I'm glad he's dead."

The lieutenant looked from Dixie to Philip and back to Dixie. He glanced at Calvin Stubbs. He shrugged.

"Let's just start at the start," he said. "It will all come out."

24

I t all came out, and it was not just a scandal but a series of scandals.

The death itself was the first subject of inquiry. Hal Kizer died alone, on New Year's Eve, in some sort of compromising position; that was all anybody knew. Where was his wife? Where were his friends? What, in fact, did he die *of,* exactly, a young man like that?

Could it be murder? No, the police said, it was not murder, so just forget about that. This was not a time for rumor or sensationalism.

Then there was the manner of his death. While reporters were still speculating on why Hal Kizer died alone on New Year's Eve, a secretary in the police department—a usually reliable source—leaked a couple details to the newspapers. He had an orange in his mouth, she had heard. An orange? How could he fit a whole orange in his mouth? And why? And—she had this on gospel authority—the body, when they found it, was nude. But then others began to volunteer information. He was nude, yes, and he had wires around his private parts and a bag over his head. These were certifiable facts, confirmed by police witnesses, who naturally wished to remain anonymous. Everyone in the press deplored the fact that the police had revealed such things; this was pure sensationalism. A reporter who kept up with the tabloids remembered a similar death in England where a Member of Parliament had killed himself, accidentally it seemed, with an orange in his mouth and panty hose tied around his neck, or something like that. Garters, maybe. He looked up the story, found it, and the newspaper ran a long feature on British Sex, and there were two newspaper editorials: "The Fall of Rome" and "The Best of Boston."

Two dedicated reporters had been looking into Hal Kizer's background, researching his private life, his family and his marriage and his work with manic-depressives, and within two days they had located Theda, who gave a lively interview, with many photos, defending her profession as an alternative lifestyle. This could all have been prevented, she said, if Hal had heeded her advice and not tried to do the British thing by himself. The British thing was particularly complicated. These were not games and they were certainly not for amateurs.

And then the real scandal: on the day of Hal's burial, word leaked that Dixie Kizer was not alone when she discovered the dead body of her husband. She was with a man, a married man. Dixie was still under heavy sedation at a private rest home and could not be reached for questioning, but rumor said that the man was Philip Tate, the new Dean of the Medical School. Reporters surrounded him after the funeral. Yes, he had been with Dixie Kizer when she found the body: he had driven her home after a New Year's open house that both she and her husband had attended, along with eighty or ninety other people from the university, and he had nothing more to say. Maggie Tate, his wife, remarked that Dixie Kizer was a family friend and a very dear and wonderful person and she too had nothing more to say. But why was Philip in the house with her when the body was found? Philip and Maggie shook their heads and looked solemn and once again had nothing more to say. Beecher Stubbs, however, suggested that Philip Tate was very probably Dixie's psychiatrist, so *of course* he wouldn't comment. Beecher's suggestion ended that line of inquiry. Nobody in an academic com-

munity wanted to appear to be violating a doctor's confidentiality. Some things were sacred.

Hal was buried and a memorial service was held and the
Tates drew a deep breath.

The reporters, however, had not yet finished. They discovered that on the night of Hal's death, Dixie Kizer had been out
nightclubbing—slumming, some might say—with a bunch of
college kids. Philip Tate's son, Cole, had been among them. This
Cole had been seen kissing Dixie Kizer. A blurry Polaroid turned
up, two people snuggling in the Oasis, and the caption read "Cole
and Dixie?" With a question mark. That was in the morning
paper. By evening there was a story exposing the truth: Philip
Tate had not been there when the body was found. Cole Tate,
Philip's son, had been there. Philip Tate's story was a cover-up.

Now there were two new scandals. The love affair between
Cole and Dixie: hunky young doctor meets jaded socialite. And
the cover-up by Philip Tate: Dean of Medical School shields
son from scandal, sinks self.

Philip wrote the President a letter of resignation and went
off with his wife for a two-week vacation at an undisclosed re-
treat. They wanted some peace and privacy.

The reporters located them in an isolated beach house in
Provincetown and interviewed them outside, stamping their feet
in the snow to keep warm. The rumor was that Philip himself
had had an affair with Dixie Kizer. Would he like to comment
on that? Philip declined. Dixie Kizer herself claimed it was so,
they said. Would he comment now? No, he said. But Maggie
had a comment. She said that it certainly was so, she had known
about it all along, it was one of those middle-aged things men
sometimes do, and women also, and it would be very nice if the
reporters went away now and let them get on with their lives.
The reporters returned with photos and an essay: "Life Support,
Wife Support." It was a long piece on Maggie Tate and other
wives in recent political history who had supported their hus-

bands through and beyond an infidelity. Was it wisdom or insecurity that made them stand by their men? Psychiatrists were divided on this. Dr. Joyce Brothers said it was sometimes one thing, sometimes another. Readers were invited to phone in their responses or, if they preferred, to use fax or E-mail. Appropriate addresses were provided.

When they returned from vacation, Philip was astonished to open an official letter from the President refusing to accept his resignation as Dean of the Medical School. Philip was a distinguished psychiatrist, the President wrote, and a man of upstanding character and moral rectitude. The Trustees joined the President in expressing every confidence in Philip as Dean. The letter was dated February 7. There was another letter, this one dated February 14—Valentine's Day—the day of the "Life Support, Wife Support" article, saying that the President had conferred with the Trustees and they had decided to accept Philip's resignation after all. The school simply could not bear another sexual scandal. Former Dean Aspergarter would step in at once and relieve Philip of all Deaconal responsibilities. They were sure Philip understood.

In early March there was a follow-up on the scandal, with the news that Emma Tate, the daughter, was a lesbian, but by this time nobody cared very much except Emma, who had recently decided she wasn't a lesbian after all and hated to be misrepresented.

It had been an exhausting few months for everybody.

Dixie Kizer was out of the rest home and was living with Calvin and Beecher Stubbs. Her house was up for sale and she refused to go back to it even to collect her clothes and jewelry. Beecher did that for her.

Dixie's therapy at McLean had been very successful. When she expressed an interest in painting, they had assigned her immediately to the fine art recovery section, where she was asked to paint her feelings, most particularly her fears and her dreams. The paintings were astonishing, whorls of whites and ochres out of which emerged colorful plants that metamorphosed into creatures that were animals and women both, seductive, tortuous, all of them in a state of becoming. They were erotic and compelling and everyone who saw them was disturbed by them. They made Dixie very happy. And because the paintings were good, people thought she must be sane.

During these difficult months Beecher and Calvin Stubbs continued on as usual. Calvin read and researched and wrote his essays. Beecher shopped with friends and lunched at Neiman Marcus and dined with Calvin on their new choice in cereal, Honey Nut Cheerios. They lived life whole and they looked after Dixie Kizer as well.

For Maggie and Philip life was different, but only for a while. By June the scandal had gone away for good, and by that time they had long since agreed not to talk about it, to let it rest. For the most part they succeeded.

And then one day, as they were cleaning the garage, Philip was suddenly stricken.

"Have I ruined everything?"

They were getting rid of household junk that Philip had not been able to part with: a lamp from his study, a computer keyboard, boxes and boxes of old drafts of articles, and offprints, and ancient tax records. He gasped for breath. He looked over at Maggie in her jeans and work shirt, a scarf around her hair, and, breathless, he felt his heart drop. He had almost lost her. She was aging, she was very beautiful, he loved her, only her. And he had never told her the truth: he had almost ruined everything by that one night ride, the break-in, and Dixie Kizer. He must have been insane.

He would tell her now. It was not the secret itself that mattered. It was what it signified: the last dark corner within, that even he himself had never penetrated. He would do it, and he would do it now.

"Have I ruined everything?" he asked.

Maggie heard the fear in his voice and turned to look at him. "Don't," she said.

"Maggie, I've never told you," he said.

She dropped the box she was holding and came to him. She put her arms around his neck and held him close and whispered, "You don't have to tell me anything. It's all right."

"You don't know what happened," he said.

But they were talking about two different things.

"No, I don't. I know that I loved you and then for a while I didn't love you, I didn't love you at all, and then I loved you again. And that's enough."

"I'm so lucky," he said, and held her for a long time.

And still he did not tell her.

FIVE

25

Dean Thurgood rose to offer a toast. "John McGuinn and his lovely wife Nancy," he said, and then he went on to enumerate their many virtues, and John's in particular, to demonstrate how right and good it was that John McGuinn should occupy the Howard K. Merk Chair of Clinical Psychology. "To John McGuinn," the Dean said, "long life, good health, our warm congratulations."

They all raised their glasses in a toast.

It was Thurgood's first anniversary as Dean of the Medical School and he took the opportunity to thank everybody at the dinner by name. He had needed their support, he said, and he was grateful for their generosity, for everybody's generosity really, but particularly for Philip Tate's. "To Philip Tate," he said, and again they all lifted their glasses in a toast.

In a few more minutes it was all over. Then good-byes and thanks and more good-byes, and Maggie and Philip Tate were in their car driving home.

"What a nice evening," Maggie said. "I'm glad for John and Nancy."

"It *was* a nice evening," Philip said.

They drove in silence, thinking.

Philip was thinking how strange life was and how wonderful. It was just over a year now, a year and a few days, since the Aspergarter dinner when he'd been toasted as the new Tyler P.

Goldman Chair of Psychiatry. His life had been a mess then, he'd been deluded and self-righteous, and Maggie had been drifting away. Now everything had been restored to him: his work, his wife, his great kids, everything. It was like something in the Old Testament, a wrestling match with an angel, a wager with God. He reached over and put his hand on Maggie's leg.

"What?" she said.

"How lucky we are."

"Keep it in mind," she said.

He patted her leg and smiled.

"How's the book coming?" he said.

"I did my two pages."

"Very good. Very good."

"I don't know if they're very good, or even half good, but I did them, and that's my promise to myself."

"You can do it," he said.

"I will," she said. "I'll do it."

Maggie was writing a novel. She wouldn't tell him what it was about except that it was not about them. The plot was a secret but, just to reassure him, she had told him this much: it concerned a woman whose life is on the skids until she has an affair with her psychiatrist, or maybe with a bartender; she hadn't decided yet. Hmm, Philip said. And it's about a man who does not know how to love. What happens to them? She wouldn't tell. She didn't know for sure, she said, and besides, if she talked about it, it might go away. She was doing two pages a day, five days a week, when she wasn't teaching. When she was teaching, she dropped the count to one page a day. She was very anxious, she said, but he could see she was happy too, insofar as anybody gets to be happy.

"I'm feeling happy," he said.

"Me too," she said.

And then they were home.

In the kitchen they had a Coke and their vitamin pills and then Maggie kissed him good night. She paused on the stairs. "Are you gonna read for a while?"

"I think so. Unwind a little."

"I'm beat," she said. "Don't wake me when you come to bed, okay?"

"Love you," he said.

"Love you," she said.

Philip poured himself another Coke and went into the study to read the newspaper. The usual stories: the decline of civilization, the end of the human race, who could care? And then, in the Arts section, he came across a notice of Dixie Kizer's one-woman show. It was being held at a museum in the Berkshires for the entire month of August. Dixie was flourishing. Why did that not surprise him? She had stalked him like a crazy person. She had wanted her husband dead. And what had come of it all? Trouble. Nothing but trouble. Dixie was one of those strange and dangerous women, the only survivor of every wreck she was in. She had her own gallery in Baltimore now and she was taken seriously by serious painters. She was taken seriously too by Cole, who lived ten minutes from her and saw her regularly. What could you do? What could anyone do? And poor old Hal was still very much dead.

Philip had thought a great deal about Hal during the past year. He had been so convinced that Hal had no inner life at all, that he was dangerous and evil, but lately he had a nagging worry that perhaps, in a peculiar way, Hal was right. Perhaps there was an inner life unknown to him, a passage through the flesh rather than above it, with an impulse that was dark and mysterious and unfathomable.

Certainly Hal had been convinced that he was on some suprarational quest, that he had some kind of hunger for ecstasy that justified being horny all the time. St. Augustine, with a twist, sort of. But at least Hal knew what he was after. Whereas, house-breaking? What was that about?

For a second, for a fraction of a second—it was like a stroke—his mind split open and he saw that Hal was right; they were alike; they were not resigned to life and then death; they wanted to get outside their skins. And then—that blow to the brain—his mind closed up, and he was back where he began.

He had broken into the Kizers' house. It was crazy. It was mad.

The Kizers' house had been bought by a new couple at the Medical School. They had been at the party tonight: an older woman, a younger man, no kids. The husband was very unhappy and the wife was knocking herself out to make him feel he mattered, and you could see it was never going to work. She was something in hospital administration. God knows what he was. He had a kind of surly expression, defying you to entertain him. Philip hadn't tried very hard, he had to admit. Still, the guy was interesting in his way. He was so obviously hurting.

Philip went into the kitchen and got a glass of water. It was a cool night, beautiful June weather; he could take a walk. Or a drive. Why not?

The sky was dark, with a sliver of moon and lots of stars. He stood in the driveway and looked up at the Big Dipper, the North Star, at Arcturus with his sword rampant. The air was clean. Everything smelled sexy.

He drove out to Harvard Square and then—amused at the idea, not in the least tempted this time—he drove over to Winchester and parked down the street from the Kizers' old house. It was very late and there were no lights on, unless there was a light in the sunroom. You couldn't see the sunroom from the street.

He could get out of the car and walk down the driveway and around the back and take a little look. What harm?

His heart began to beat faster. It was silly. It was crazy, really. Think of the past year. He felt sick to his stomach but he went ahead anyway.

He got out of the car and walked slowly down the drive and around the back of the house. There seemed to be a light in the sunroom, but because of the garden wall, he couldn't be sure. His heart was beating very fast now. He moved quickly to the door and ran his hand along the top of the frame. The key was there. He slipped it in the lock and turned the knob. He could walk in. He could walk through the house, just looking, not touching, a quiet, secret, harmless night visit.

He paused, the door ajar, ready to enter.

"Maggie," he said, and he did not know if he said it out loud or merely to himself.

Instantly he pulled the door closed, removed the key, and put it back above the door. He went out to his car and got in. He drove home.

His heart was racing now. He was going to have a heart attack, a stroke, something. He parked the car in the driveway— he did not have time to mess around with the garage.

He got out of the car, quickly, quickly, and started toward the house.

If she was still awake, he would tell her right now. He would tell her who he was and what he had done. He would wake her and tell her.

It was his only hope for salvation.

He approached the house running, a man possessed.